Spring Comes to World's End

Monica Dickens, the great-granddaughter of Charles Dickens, now lives with her husband and two children in America, surrounded by horses, cats and dogs. Author of the famous *One Pair of Hands* and *One Pair of Feet*, autobiographies of her early life, she has written such successful novels as *Kate and Emma* and is also the author of *Follyfoot* and *Dora at Follyfoot*, bestsellers published in Piccolo.

Also published in Piccolo are her three previous books in the World's End series: *The House at World's End*, *Summer at World's End* and *World's End in Winter*.

Monica Dickens

Spring comes to World's End

Cover illustration by Peter Charles
Text illustrations by Gareth Floyd

A Piccolo book
Pan Books in association with
William Heinemann Ltd

First published 1973 by William Heinemann Ltd
This edition published 1975 by Pan Books Ltd,
Cavaye Place, London SW10 9PG,
in association with William Heinemann Ltd
ISBN 0 330 24376 4
© Monica Dickens 1973

The author and publishers are indebted
to the Guide Dogs for the Blind Association
for their help and advice

Printed in Great Britain by
Richard Clay (The Chaucer Press) Ltd, Bungay, Suffolk

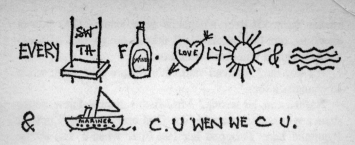

EVERY SW TH F WINE. LOVE LY ☀ & ≈≈

& MARINER. C. U WEN WE C. U.

one

When the postcard came from the Mediterranean, Carrie and Michael rode down the lane to show it to Mr Mismo.

He was out in the pigsties behind his barn, leaning over the low wall, in silent communion with an enormous sow.

'Howdy.' Mr Mismo had been watching Westerns on television this winter. 'Fall off and stay awhile.'

Carrie got off John and joined him by the wall. 'What's wrong with Pygmalia?'

'Same as usual.' The enormous sow, famous for motherhood, lay on her side panting gently, bristly lids closed over small eyes. You could see the babies heaving about inside her. 'Any day now.'

Mr Mismo turned his head to inspect Carrie's brown horse John from under the brim of his green hat, then travelled his shrewd horsey gaze to Oliver Twist, who was lipping up scattered chicken feed and shedding white

5

winter hairs all over Michael's blue jeans. 'That pony's shedding out too quick. He'll take a cough one of these sharp nights if you don't watch out.'

'It's not me,' Michael said. 'It's Nature tells them when to change clothes.'

'Nature can be wrong.' Mr Mismo always knew better than anyone, even people like God and Nature. 'Look at Pygmalia here. Dropped her last litter when I was at the Agricultural Banquet, and the old fool rolled over and crushed four piglets.'

'Don't remind me.' Carrie had come down to feed the farm animals for Mr Mismo, and found the dreadful holocaust. 'Look, we got a card from Mother and Dad.'

Elbows on the brick wall, Mr Mismo pushed out his lip and puzzled over the postcard. He was no good at hieroglyphics. Even when Carrie explained the pictures, he still said, 'A bottle of wine, eh? I thought it was always beer with your father.'

'It means *fine*, not wine,' Michael said. 'It's higlophobics.'

'And that's Mother, see.' Carrie pointed. 'She's First Mate – well, she cooks actually, and Dad is the Captain. It's a charter yacht in the Mediterranean, I told you. Millionaires hire it by the week and have great parties and fall overboard.'

'Because of the wine bottle.' Mr Mismo, who knew everything known about horses, and many things not known, because he made them up, would never understand the postcard. 'But I'd not have thought a free soul like your Dad would hire himself out to anybody, let alone a millionaire.'

'But this is a crisis, you know it is. If we can't raise the money to buy World's End, Uncle Rudolf will sell the house and land to a developer, and turn us out. That's why Dad took this job.'

'He'll never stick it.'

Having settled that, Mr Mismo turned back to the pig, and scratched her heaving side gently with the end of his stick.

Uncle Rudolf said the same thing when he stopped in at World's End a few days later.

'We heard from Dad,' Carrie told him. 'They love the job on the yacht.'

'For how long?' Uncle Rudolf always raised his thin eyebrows and dropped his pouty lower lip when he spoke of his brother. 'He'll never stick it.'

'He's got to,' Carrie said grimly, 'to buy World's End from you.'

'Listen, child,' Uncle Rudolf said, 'if I waited for your father to raise the money, I'd die of old age.'

'Then you could leave us the house in your will, Uncle Rhubarb,' Michael said brightly.

'Don't call me that. I've just seen the estate agent. He tells me the property may turn out to be worth a good bit more than I thought.'

We always knew that.

When Uncle Rudolf let Tom and Carrie and Em and Michael move into World's End, he thought it was a useless ruin. But they had always known, even before they patched it up and made it liveable, that it was a priceless treasure.

'That's why Mother and Dad are working so hard,' Carrie said.

'Hard work and your father,' Uncle Rudolf smiled coldly, with his mouth, not his eyes, 'are like two parallel lines. They never come together.'

'Good thing he doesn't know about the school burning down,' Michael said when Rudolf had driven off in his shiny black car which looked like a hearse. 'He'd tell

Mother and Dad, to make them worry about us.'

'Hoping they'd chuck the job and come home,' Carrie said, 'to prove him right.'

The school had caught fire last week in the middle of Assembly, cutting short one of Mrs Loomis's lectures on vandalism of school property:

'But some of you people don't seem to know the meaning of the word consideration for—'

'Fire!'

All the bells went off. It was just like Fire Drill, except that everyone ran out instead of walking, and Miss McDrane had hysterics in the playground, and Michael dashed a bucket of water over her shoes. Carrie took John out of the baker's stable next door, and led him off to the other side of the nail factory, where he could not smell the smoke.

'The second fire in my lifetime.' Michael wanted to tell about the night his first home had burned down to a skeleton of charred beams and chimney stack. But everyone was too excited to listen, thrilled and scared at the same time by the spurts of flame and the billowing smoke, as the fire ate into the familiar things of every day. When the roof over the Detention Room crashed in under a torrent of water, a great sound, half sigh, half groan, went up from the children watching in the cricket field, although everyone had hated the Detention Room and spent unhappy times there.

But it was a part of my past, thought Carrie's younger sister Em, sheltering the school cat under her jacket. *A part of my childhood.*

Goodby to all that, said the other voice in her head, which talked back to her in dialogue, like in a play.

She took the grey cat home, since no one looked for it. It had been named Silver at school, but Em called it Joan of Arc, because it would have been burned alive if she had not nipped down to the boiler room and rescued it.

'That makes a hundred and thirty-five legs.' Michael had chalked a long sum on the floor to count up the animals and people at World's End, as they sat up late playing cards, because they would not have to go to school tomorrow. It was not a complete pack of cards. Nothing at World's End was complete or unbroken. Everything was cracked, chipped, leaky, patched up, propped up, and tied together with string. But it was theirs.

'No wait.' Michael rubbed at the chalk with the frayed sleeve of his jersey. 'A hundred and thirty nine legs, if Joan of Art stays.'

'She stays.' Em had the silver cat on her lap, because the other cats had not yet accepted her. 'As long as we do. He couldn't – I mean, he never would—'

'Shut up,' Tom said. They could not speak about Rudolf selling the house and turning them out. It was unspeakable.

'But what would happen to all the animals if Uncle Rudolf—'

'Shut *up*.' Carrie clapped a hand over Em's mouth, and Em bit it. 'Don't even talk about it.'

Sucking the toothmarks out of her hand, Carrie saw an image of a long, sad trail of refugees ... horses, dogs, cats, chickens, the goat, the donkey ... animals who had found shelter here, turned out, wandering homeless.

two

Everyone had a project to raise money for the house fund in the red flour crock, that hung from a rafter in the kitchen.

When they had been saving to mend the barn roof, it had been labelled 'RAISING THE ROOF'. Now Michael had scrubbed that out, and painted 'SAVVING WORLD END'.

They all sat round the table under the crock with one hand on their chests and a lighted candle end in the other, and swore an oath:

'I swear on the honour of this dear house and land that I will not touch this money for ordinary things.'

But if there was a crisis, like an oat bill, or the soles of someone's last pair of shoes finally separated from the uppers, or the butcher saying, 'No more credit', someone would have to climb guiltily on to the kitchen table and fish for cash in the hanging crock. A hundred and thirty-nine legs was thirty-eight two-legged and four-legged mouths to feed. All too often there was a crisis.

Tom, who was the eldest, worked in the zoo hospital, taking care of sick animals, and babies whose mothers had died or rejected them. The pay wasn't much, because he was getting free training, so he took odd jobs in the evening.

At the moment, he was painting the inside of a bungalow for a couple who were going to be married. He went off to the village after supper, and came back late, with paint in his long thick hair. The bride-to-be was very fussy. She was marrying late in life, and the love nest had to be perfect now that she had finally got it. If Tom made streaks or dribbles, she made him paint the whole wall again.

'No wonder she had such a hard time getting a husband,' Tom grumbled to Carrie, who had stayed up late to make tea and muffins for him, and to feed the baby kinkajou. 'Who'd marry *her*?'

'Only Mr Evans.' The bridegroom was the pernickety chemist, who sniggered at his own rotten jokes and counted pills twice, to make sure he didn't give you one too many. 'And who would marry *him*?'

'They're welcome to each other,' Tom groaned. 'Them and their aquamarine boudoir.'

'Who will you marry?' Carrie asked.

'Nobody.'

'Not even Liza?'

'God, no.' Tom stretched out on the sagging sofa. The white cat Maud jumped on to his stomach and kneaded it, like bread dough. 'Liza and I know each other too well.' Paul, the black half-Siamese, dropped down from the dresser shelf and settled in Tom's paint-matted hair on the arm of the sofa. The shaggy dog Charlie came over and licked muffin butter off his chin.

The baby kinkajou was in a box on the kitchen table, with a toy rabbit for company. Carrie had just given him his feed, and he was asleep between the rabbit's woolly paws with his tiny pink hands curled, and his long tail coiled like the inside of a conch shell.

His mother had been ill and had no milk, and since there was no one in the zoo hospital to give four-hourly feeds at night, Tom brought him home after work.

'Who'll do the three o'clock feed?' Tom mumbled, almost asleep.

''Em said she would. She banged her head three times on the pillow.'

The only clock at World's End was a turnip watch that hung on a nail in the kitchen. The morning alarm was the rooster, Eric the Red, or John calling Carrie from the stable or field, or a dog barking to get out or in, or a cat jumping on to your face.

11

A motor bike roared down the lane, extra loud in the stillness of the night, and stopped. Voices shouted. Liza's boots ran up the front path which was made of millstones, jumping from stone to stone, crunched round the side gravel path, kicked open the back door and brought her in, with her wild red hair like a bramble bush.

'My feet are murdering me.' She dropped down on the floor where she was, and began to unlace her long boots. They were cracked and split, the leather on the toes worn away, but she wore them every day because she loved them. Good thing she did, since they were the only shoes she had. With Liza, it was boots or barefoot.

Liza Jones lived with them at World's End and worked for Alec Harvey, the vet in Newtown, except when she was in a mood to wander.

Born to trouble, as some people are born to paint in oils or play the violin, Liza went off into a rage or into the blue without warning, broke things, threw things, and insulted fussy customers with toy dogs. Not the dogs, because it was not their fault they had been degraded into ribboned playthings, fed on chicken breast and chocolates.

Alec Harvey was always threatening to sack her, but he never did. Last time she disappeared, he got really fed up, but she turned up from nowhere in the nick of time to sew up a cut artery, and save the life of a blind man's Guide Dog.

To help the fund in the red crock, she worked some nights at the Transport Café on the main road. It was the cook who had brought her home on his motor bike.

'He's getting very fresh,' Liza said, 'but it's better than hitch-hiking, and he's not as bad as some of them long-distance drivers.' She whistled. 'Language!'

'What do they say?' Carrie did not know much language, except what Liza used.

'Nothing that I can't handle, ducky.' Liza took some

folded notes out of her boot. 'Pay night. Put this in the bank.'

Carrie stood on the table and reached up to drop the notes into the flour crock. There was too long a drop until they hit bottom.

'Will it ever be full?' She crouched to tickle the full stomach of the kinkajou, who yawned his pink gums like a miniature baby. The black cat Paul jumped up with a questioning mew, and she fixed the piece of netting over the box. Paul was interested, not in the baby, but in his bowl of cereal in a corner of the box. If no one was looking, he would hang a paw over the side and scoop it up, like a cat fishing in a stream. 'Will the crock ever be full, Liza?'

'Not till we fill it.' Liza got the other boot off and flung it into the opposite corner from where she had flung the other one.

'That'll be never.'

three

Carrie was the worst money maker of all. She was no good at anything profitable. All the things she was good at were things for which no one would pay you, like riding, and writing poems.

She had tried to get weekend work mucking out at the Ups'ndowns riding stable at Newtown, but there were too many horse-mad girls who would do it for nothing to get free rides. Carrie wanted money. She didn't want free rides on the sad, submissive horses who were broken-spirited from too much work and too little food and love.

She got kicked out of the stable anyway, before she ever picked up a manure fork, for observing to the square-jawed owner, who was either a man or a woman, that the bay thoroughbred was gone over at the knees.

At school, she had earned a bit of money staying late to clean up the lab with the chemistry teacher, but the school was closed now, what was left of it, and the lab blown up with its own exploding chemicals.

She had sold horse manure round the Newtown housing estates, with John pulling the muck cart, and done a little business boarding cats and dogs when their owners went away.

But the Newtown gardeners were finding out that they could get their fertilizer free from Squarejaw at Ups'ndowns, and a Persian cat which Carrie had boarded had stayed up a tree for two days, with Charlie and Perpetua and Moses and silly Harry taking turns to bark underneath.

Mrs Loomis the headmistress had entrusted Carrie with her small white poodle, which wore a jewelled collar, slept on a foam rubber pillow, and ate mince and boiled fish, which Mrs Loomis brought over with little Snowflake.

The back of her car had hardly disappeared round the corner of the hawthorn hedge when Paul had swiped the plaice on to the floor, and a crowd of cats were growling over it, and Jake ran off with the package of mince in his mouth, turning and twisting in and out of rooms, round furniture and under and over beds, with Charlie and Harry after him.

Carrie had fed Snowflake on ham gristle and new-laid eggs and the turnips no one would eat in Liza's stew, and Mrs Loomis was ecstatic with how well the little dog looked. She recommended Carrie to a textbook salesman who was going to the Isle of Man for a business conference.

The salesman brought a gaunt animal called Gilbert, part wolfhound, part Dane, and part greyhound, from the size of his slender waist. He ate everything he could lay his jaws on, including an arithmetic book, three shoes, Em's knitting, and the only decent leather halter they had.

The book salesman never collected him. Mrs Loomis found out from his firm that he had settled down with a rich widow in the Isle of Man, and was never coming back. So Gilbert stayed, and went on eating.

A hundred and forty-three legs. Thirty-nine mouths.

'I'd count up the teeth,' Michael said, 'if I could add in the thousands.'

The trouble with Carrie was that when she took in money, it usually went out before it got to the red crock.

She gave some riding lessons to a ham-fisted boy with legs like beer bottles – on his own pony, since she would never teach on John. She was on the table, reaching up to put the teaching money into the crock, when the Cruelty Man turned up with a scarred and wobbly little donkey he had found on a building site with a can tied to the tuft of his tail, and boys shooting bows and arrows at him.

'Carrie, could you possibly—'

'Oh, *yes*.'

Carrie called the donkey Sebastian, after the saint who was tied to a tree and martyred with arrows. She put him in the orchard with Leonora, the grey jenny who had also suffered at the hands of Man, before she found refuge at World's End.

Carrie had to buy a sickle to cut grass for Sebastian, because his front teeth were too bad to graze, and she spent almost all the teaching money on vitamins and bran for him, and zinc ointment for his sores.

Now that there was no school to take up her time, she was making deliveries for the grocer, with John in the trap. So far she had earned nothing, because they owed the grocer money, and he was paying himself back out of Carrie's wages.

four

Michael, the youngest of the Fielding family, made a little money for the flour crock by selling inventions and constructions. But most of the local people who were willing to buy his trivets and stools and shopping baskets and birdhouses had already bought them.

He tried to get repeat sales.

'You've got two cars, Mrs Wassername. Why not be a two-birdhouse family?'

Or: 'If you bought another stool, Mr Beastly, you could put it on the other side of the fireplace and make conversation.'

'The first one broke,' Mr Peasly said, 'and we put it on the fire.'

'Well then, you need another.'

'No ta, Michael.'

He was currently working on an ingenious method for making trays out of old picture frames, or picture frames out of trays, whichever the public wanted.

'Would you like one?' He took it out to the lane when Mrs Potter came to collect Em for baby-sitting.

'One what, dear?'

'One afternoon tea tray.'

'It looks like a picture frame.'

'It was, but—'

The middle Potter child, who had a face like Man before he evolved from the apes, reached through the car window, snatched up the tray and banged it down over Michael's head. The middle fell out, and it was a frame again, with Michael's head as the picture.

When the warmer weather came, Miss Cordelia Chattaway would pay him small amounts to take her for rides in the rickety wicker carriage, drawn by his pony Oliver, and to push her to church in her wheelchair, and find the hymns for her, and prod her awake if she snored during the sermon.

Until then, he earned the money doing her shopping, and reading aloud to her in the evenings by the feeble light of one of the dim-watted bulbs which were as much as her watery old eyes could stand in her cottage.

She paid him out of a biscuit tin in penny and two pence pieces. Bessie Munce at the Post Office was very irritable about changing them into silver, so Michael was saving them up until he got up enough nerve to take them to the Post Office.

No teacher had ever been able to make Michael read like other people. No one could understand him when he read aloud, but Miss Chattaway couldn't understand much anyway, so it didn't matter.

Michael was reading Shakespeare to her. She had said, 'Just take a book down from the shelf dear, any book will do.' Michael had taken down *Julius Caesar,* because it had a red leather binding with gold on the edges of the paper. When you opened it, you dropped your nose into a marvellous old smell like stored apples, and mushrooms, and attics on rainy days.

'Fiends, Roomans, cutterymen, lend me your hears;
I come to buy Kassar, not to prize him.
The level that men do life after them;'
The good is soft untired wit three boons;
So let it be wit Kassar.'

'That's very lovely.' Miss Chattaway sighed, and dabbed at her weak eyes. 'It reminds me of those good old days at Bournemouth when we had the garden parties and the dear Bishop sang.'

She remembered things at random, not for any reason.

Little doors in the back of her mind opened, and out came Bournemouth, or the dear Bishop.

Her chow dog Lancelot slept on her feet, twitching and giving out little senile yelps. Presently Miss Chattaway slept too, the tissue paper folds of her chin dropped on to the lace modesty vest she pinned inside the neck of her dress.

'When that the paw have crid, Kassar hat weeped;
Amption sold be mad of strainer stoof.'

Michael read doggedly on, until the church clock struck eight-thirty.

'My health is in the coughing there wit Kassar,
And I must puze till it come bike to me.'

Michael shut the book with a bang which released some mildewy dust. Miss Chattaway woke.

'Ah, the Bible, the good word.' She had no idea what he had been reading. 'The food of the soul.'

She and Michael had sugared milk and gingerbread, and then he ran home down the lane under the cold stars, with bony, bounding Gilbert to protect him.

Em could always make a bit of money baby-sitting. She had a good local reputation, because she washed up, as well as watching television, so she could pick and choose who she would go to. But in this crisis, she went to the people who paid her the most, which was the people with the nastiest children.

Mrs Potter paid her danger money whenever the youngest child bit her hard enough to draw blood. Mrs Riley, who had run through every baby-sitter in the neighbourhood, paid Em double rates if she would feed her two-year-old, which threw spoons and plates all over the room, and emptied dishes of spinach on its head.

When you did manage to get some food down it, it waited in the high chair while you rinsed the bowl and mug, then sicked the whole meal up over you when you came to lift it down.

The night when Em banged her head three times for the kinkajou's three o'clock feed, she woke in the middle of a dream of fame, and came downstairs, with the applause still filling her ears, to see that it was exactly three o'clock. Tom was asleep on the sofa. The kinkajou was awake, and crying like a kitten.

Its bottle was in a pan of warm water at the back of the stove. Em unfastened the netting, wrapped the tiny naked body in a towel, and cradled him on her lap while she fed him. He sucked quietly, grabbing the bottle with his tiny hands. Em went back to sleep, trying to pick up the dream where it had left off, with the single scarlet rose flung on to the stage at her feet.

She woke with a start to find that she was holding the bottle and feeding nothing. The kinkajou had slipped off her lap. Charlie, who adored tiny things, had taken him out of the towel and carried him under the table, where he was licking him gently, with his eyes half closed.

'Sorry, Charlie.' Em took the kinkajou away from between his hairy paws, dried him, and took him upstairs in the box to her room at the top of the house.

Tom did not open an eye. He slept like a dead soldier, one leg on the sofa and the other sprawled on the floor, his head tipped back on his long thin neck, and his Adam's apple like a golf ball.

At seven o'clock, he woke, and climbed the twisting stair to the linen cupboard where Em slept on a mattress on a shelf, to feed the kinkajou and take him to the zoo for the day.

'Get up, Em.'

She rolled over and kicked out at him. 'Go away. There's no school.'

'Some people—' Tom threw a towel over her head – 'get all the luck.'

five

But the luck did not last. They thought they would have
a holiday until Easter at least, but an official told them
cheerfully, as if it was good news, that they must go to the
big glass-walled school at Newtown.

It was too far to drive every day with John and the trap.
They walked through the wood to the crossroads and caught
the bus that Liza took to work at the vet's.

She usually rode to the bus stop on the ancient clanking
bicycle, but now she let the others take turns on it and
start a bit later. Not that it went much faster than walking,
because the chain came off if you pedalled too hard.

Michael could not reach the pedals, so he fastened
blocks of wood to them with baling wire, the left block
bigger, because his left leg was shorter than the right, or
his right leg was longer than the left, whichever way you
wanted to look at it.

Em's legs were short too, but Liza and Carrie had to ride
with their knees up to their chins, pedalling lopsidedly up
to the bus stop and flinging the bike behind the hedge just
as the bus came round the corner, full of morning-faced
people going to work in the factories outside Newtown.

It was hard to change from the small, familiar school where
life had gone slowly and you could be yourself, to this
bustling new place full of strangers who did not know your
name.

Michael would not risk writing his, because he had ten
different ways of spelling it, and all of them were wrong.

Em went back to calling herself Esmeralda, her professional baby-sitting name which she used to impress new
customers.

Carrie started herself off as Caroline, but since no one had ever called her that, she didn't answer to it, and the teacher thought she was deaf.

On the third day, a platoon of ants marched out of her duffle bag, which had been on a shelf in the kitchen, where ants were coming to life at the end of the winter.

What was wrong with ants? They were clean and hardworking, which was more than you could say for most people. No one at the country school would have turned a hair, but this class of town-dwellers hooted and shrieked, and Mrs Flack told Carrie to scoop the ants off her desk and shake her bag out of the window into the rain.

'Ants hate rain.'

'How do you know?'

Mrs Flack was young and interested, with hair cut shorter than a boy, but Carrie could not say that her friend Lester knew, because he had been an insect in some earlier life.

She had been laughed at once that morning, the laughter that is tongues of fire, shrivelling you to nothing.

So she did not answer, and Mrs Flack still thought she was deaf.

But on that third day, the last class was Music, and life looked up again and gave Carrie the nod.

Because she could not face the crowd in the playground, she went early into the small school theatre. The teacher was sitting on the edge of the stage, with his shoes off and his bearded chin in his hands, singing softly to himself and looking at nothing.

Carrie came in and stood by the door, not wanting to disturb him.

'Who-who's that?' he asked. He had a slight stammer.

'Carrie Fielding.' She was not going to call herself

Caroline, and risk being thought deaf in a singing class. 'I'm new.'

'Wel-wel—'

He screwed up his mouth and eyes. They were ordinary looking eyes. But then Carrie saw the big yellow labrador asleep on a folded rug by the piano on stage. It was the guide dog whose life Liza had saved by stitching up the cut leg herself, at night.

'Wendy!' she said, and the blind man finally got out, 'Welcome!' at the same time, and they both laughed. He had an odd gasping laugh, mostly inside himself, as if he were not used to laughing out loud with someone else.

'I saw your dog when she was at the vet's.' Carrie climbed on stage and knelt to stroke the heavy, loose-skinned dog, who opened one amber eye, thumped her tail twice, licked her lips three times, swallowed and went back to sleep. The long scar on her front leg had healed, but the silky hair was still shorter where Liza had shaved round the wound.

'I'm Roger Wil-Wilson.'

He seemed rather shy of Carrie. A grown-up shy of a child? Carrie had thought that one of the few decent things about growing up would be losing shyness.

'Do you know,' he asked, 'at the vet's, a girl called Li-Li—?'

'Liza? She's our friend.'

'Oh then, I – then will you—'

The class came pouring in like water. Mr Wilson got up and took refuge on the piano stool, as the girls swarmed on stage and smothered Wendy with cries of love and admiration, pushing Carrie out of the way. The boys went to the last rows of the theatre and read comics, with their feet on the backs of the seats in front.

Roger Wilson did not mind what they did, as long as they either sang or kept quiet. Three of the boys played

24

cards on a brief case on their laps. Some of the girls sat on the floor of the stage and searched their long hair for split ends.

Mr Wilson's fingers went quickly over a large sheet of music on the piano. It was Braille, with raised dots for the music and the words. As his fingers moved, he hummed, as if he were reading the music. He was. His fingers were his eyes.

Then he played the piano while the class sang, still lounging about, as if they were at a party.

Carrie didn't sing at first, but then she joined in the last sad verse of the folk song.

'I once had a doggie
To walk on by my side,
But a dog catcher got ahold of him,
And he ain't no more mine.'

At the end, Roger Wilson looked in Carrie's direction and said uncertainly, 'Was someone a bit flat?'

He sang the end of the song:

'Now I am a-living,
But someday I will die,
Some kind soul will bury me,
Put flowers by my side.'

He had the kind of voice which sends little shivers up your spine, like a finger rubbed round the top of a glass. He didn't stammer when he sang.

Then he played the piano for them, and some of the girls danced, jerking about in one spot. It wasn't like a lesson at all. He sat on the floor with Wendy and played the guitar and sang, 'Where Have All the Flowers Gone?'

Afterwards when the others had rushed out, leaving the theatre like an empty rain barrel, he told Carrie, 'I'm glad you are a friend of Li-Li—'

'Liza.' When people stammered, did they want you to help them or not?

'When I'm glad, I like sad songs.'

'Me too.' Carrie lived gladly, of course, like everyone at World's End, rubbing along somehow without grown-ups or ever enough money or food; but with horses, cats, dogs, a goat and a sheep, chickens, ducks, rabbits, a donkey, a guineapig, and wild mice in the feed shed who made jokes about the cats.

But if World's End was sold to someone else, if they lost it all ... Carrie knew that she would never be glad about anything again.

Roger Wilson sat down to put on his shoes, and Wendy got up, shook herself and jumped down from the stage, waving her tail.

'You've got a hole in your sock,' Carrie said, not critically, because socks with holes were the only kind she had, but helpfully, in case he didn't know.

His cheeks blushed between the fringe of soft beard which framed his mild face like brown animal fur. 'I forgot to darn it.'

'Do you live alone?'

'No. With Wendy.'

He put on the lead and harness and the dog stood alert, like a horse who may lounge about in his stable or field, but looks quite different tacked up for work in his saddle and bridle.

Carrie opened the door, and the man and dog set off down the corridor so fast that she almost had to run to keep up with them.

'Will you tell Li-Li—' he said, 'that I did buy her some socks.'

The night the drunk had thrown the bottle that cut Wendy's leg, Liza had ruined a sock by using it for a tourniquet.

'Why didn't you give them to her?'

Carrie had heard Liza grumble to Em, 'Men. They're all the same, blind or not. Promise you a diamond necklace or a pair of socks, and that's the last you hear of it.'

'Cast you aside like a broken doll,' Em had quoted from one of her own plays.

'Wendy hates to go to the vet's,' Mr Wilson said, 'and I didn't know where Li-Li-Li—' he gave up. 'Where she lives.'

'She lives with us. At World's End.'

'World's what?' They were at the big glass doors which led to outside.

'End,' Carrie said. 'It's an old inn. Well, it was once, but now it's where we live, my brother Tom, he works at the zoo, and Liza, and Em and Michael who are in this school somewhere – I haven't seen them since we came – and thousands of animals.'

'Hor-horses?' When Mr Wilson smiled, his small teeth glimmered very white through his soft brown beard.

'You like them?'

He nodded. 'So does Wendy. She was a puppy at a place with horses.'

'We've got three – well, one's a pony. I wish we had more. We will some day. If you are a horse fool, they – sort of come to you. Like Peter did. He ran away from a wicked girl. And John. I rescued him from the slaughterhouse. You wouldn't believe what he looked like then. He's filled out so, and got a strong crest on his neck, and his quarters have really muscled up, because he uses his back properly when he jumps.'

Mr Wilson listened with both ears, not a quarter of one ear, as most people did when Carrie gave horse lectures. They walked together through the door and down the steps and across the car park, while she elaborated on the wonders of John.

'Look out!' A car backed out, and she put out a hand to grab the blind man, but Wendy had already halted, to stop him.

'Stupid clot!' Carrie made a face at the back of the departing car, which held the Assistant Headmaster, very upright, with a hat at dead centre.

'No. I tell them not to watch out for me. Wendy might think all drivers would, and get careless. We watch out for them.' He used words like 'watch' and 'see', as if he had working eyes. Carrie shouldn't have grabbed him and yelled.

At the busy main road, she said, 'I go across here for my bus, if you're all right.'

Wrong again. If he wasn't all right without Carrie, what would be the point of the guide dog?

'I cross here too.'

When most dogs sit, they bring their front feet back to their hindquarters. Wendy brought her quarters up to her front legs, to stay beside him. She sat at the edge of the kerb and watched and listened. Roger Wilson listened. They waited for quite a long time. Should Carrie offer help? She had never known a blind person before.

She was just going to say, 'It's safe now,' when he told the dog, 'Forward!' at just the right time, and they went across the busy road in a space between the traffic, stepped on to the pavement, and turned smartly left between a pram and a lamp post. Carrie ran after them and was nearly run down by a bicycle.

Mr Wilson stopped at the bus shelter to say goodbye. The street was full of people and traffic noise. On a building site, huge drills chattered, and a bulldozer shovelled lumps of concrete.

'Lucky you,' he raised his voice, 'going back to World's Whatsit.'

'Why don't you come out some time?' Carrie said impulsively. 'You could bring Liza's socks.'

'Cou-could I?' He looked at Carrie eagerly, as if he really could see her.

'Come on Saturday. Liza's making brandy snaps.'

She told him which bus to take into the country, and where to get off. She knew by now that she need not offer to meet him at the bus stop.

She said, 'You turn left, walk about half a mile down a lane through a wood like a tunnel, that drips on you – rain and caterpillars – and when you come out, it's the first house on the left at the bend in the lane. There's a gate. Follow the smell of horses, and I'll be in the stable.'

The bus came.

'Bring your holey socks too!' Carrie shouted above the traffic and the bulldozer. 'Em will darn them!'

six

He brought six pairs of socks wrapped in a shirt that needed buttons. He came walking fast round the bend of the lane, with Wendy moving steadily ahead, not getting sidetracked by smells and movements in the hedge. She was the first dog to come down that lane, on or off a lead, without making a lunge and a yelping scrabble at the rabbit burrow under the corner oak.

Carrie saw them from the stableyard, where she was wheeling a loaded barrow out to the manure heap.

Mr Wilson stopped with his head up, like a dog getting the scent. Then he said something to Wendy, and she turned left across the lane. He spoke to her all the time. 'Inside, Wendy,' he was telling her. 'Inside.'

She led him off the lane, looking back at him to see if she was right, and stopped by the gate.

'Good girl.' He felt his way along it until he found the latch, opened it, came through, and Wendy stopped as he turned back to shut it. Carrie called, and they came more slowly across the uneven ground of the yard, stepping neatly round the hollows where the chickens took dust baths, and the mounting block which Michael had made from the top of a broken stepladder, because his pony was too broad to jump on bareback.

Carrie brought out John, well groomed, so that he would feel clean and silky. Roger Wilson went all over him with his gentle musician's hands, and laid his bearded face against John's neck to breathe in the smell of him with great pleasure.

He kept talking to Wendy, so that she would not be jealous, and Carrie talked to Charlie, so that he wouldn't mind a strange dog in his stable yard.

He had barked from the top of the wall as they approached, but Wendy paid no attention, because she was on duty. Charlie jumped down to inspect her harness carefully, then watched with interest while she and the man, who seemed to be part of each other, worked their way among the obstacles in the yard. Charlie had been a professional television star, famous for dog biscuit commercials; but here was a branch of business he didn't know.

While Mr Wilson was stroking John, Wendy sat in front of the horse grinning, with the handle of her harness on her back, and her ears pricked as far as labrador ears will go. Dogs and horses don't often talk together, except by unseen thoughts, but John dropped his nose, Wendy raised hers, and they exchanged some kind of message.

Charlie went back to the top of the wall with some of the cats to watch the lane for the travelling fish van, whose driver threw out a package of free cods' heads on Saturdays without even slowing down.

When Carrie had shown Mr Wilson the other animals, she took him into the house. Henry the ram, who thought he was a dog, almost knocked him down shouldering past him through the door. Before he could get thrown out again, the ram lay down with a grunt in front of the stove, tucking his hard little hoofs under him.

Liza was kneading dough on a piece of cupboard door which Tom had cut up for a bread board.

'Hullo, Rodge,' she said, as if she had seen him yesterday.

'Hullo, Li-Li—' He stood smiling shyly by the door, and Wendy waited by his legs to see which way they would go across the floor, where Henry was a mound of grubby wool, and Carrie's saddle sat over a stool, and the sofa was upside down, because someone had been looking for a

31

mislaid kitten among the springs and torn stuffing. 'I got the socks. Red, to go with your hair.'

'My hair ain't purple.' Liza threw down the satiny ball of dough and came over, as he took the socks out of his pocket. 'If they sold you those as red, you've been had, Rodge.' She knelt to Wendy. 'How's the leg, girl? The scar looks good.'

'It was a wonderful job,' Roger Wilson said.

'Well.' Liza tucked back her thick red hair and left a strand of dough in it. 'Look who done it.'

They had tea and Liza's brandysnaps, rolled into cones round a carrot, and Rodge carved his initials on the big round table which was their visitors' book, feeling along the letters with his fingers. They all called him Rodge, as if he was not a teacher.

After that, he came quite often to World's End. He was not so shy when he was there, and he didn't stammer. He still could not say 'Liza', so he gave it up and called her Girl.

When he had learned his way about the house and garden and the stables and barn, he did odd jobs. He dug the vegetable patch, and put in some cabbage seedlings. He mended a broken cane chair with glue and string. He cleaned horses and tack with Carrie. He swept floors with Em, and made scones. He helped Michael to build a triangular chicken coop, which somehow came out with four sides.

Wendy lay close to him, to be there when he needed her, and he talked to her a lot, because a Guide Dog must never be an independent dog on its own. The partnership must always stay close. But often, because she was a dog as well as a guide dog, Rodge let her go free with the others, running and tracking all over the hill field and the thicket, but coming back at once to his whistle.

He brought his guitar and taught Liza some chords.

'You've got natural hands for it, girl,' he told her.

'Knock it off.' Liza fiercely rejected praise. 'I got natural hands for work, that's all.' She looked at them. The nails were only clean because the part that got dirty was bitten off. 'Good thing you can't see 'em, Rodge. These hands done everything but murder.'

Rodge did not much like his cramped flat in Newtown, where his landlady did not bother about him, except to call up the stairs, 'Everything all right, Mr W.?' just when he had gone to sleep.

She cooked for him occasionally, when she was at home, which was not often, because she was in Politics. Rodge seemed to exist mostly on hardboiled eggs and baked beans and frozen dinners. He read Braille, and listened to radio music and talking books on a tape recorder. He did not seem to have many friends. Because of Wendy, he said he wasn't lonely, but they thought he was.

Sometimes he stayed the night at World's End. He caught the afternoon bus home with them, and the early one to school next morning, walking so fast with Wendy that he could start out almost as late as whoever was riding the bicycle.

It was fun at school, calling him Mr Wilson with a straight face, hiding the secret of being his friend, because it wasn't done to be too chummy with the teachers.

The school claimed Wendy as 'their' dog. She figured as mascot in all the class and team photographs, and everyone was saving milk bottle tops for the guide dog fund.

But at World's End, she was just one of the dogs. She lay under the kitchen table with Charlie, his shaggy head hanging over a cross bar, her golden muzzle on Rodge's sock, while he played the guitar and sang after supper. Rodge could not make music with his shoes on.

And upstairs in the room where a tree's budding twigs

tapped at the window, Rodge slept on the good mattress they had bought for Mother when her back was bad, and Wendy slept on John's folded winter rug, which Carrie had made from oat sacks and an old khaki blanket from Mr Mismo's army days.

seven

One weekend, Jan Lynch, Tom's boss at the zoo, took home the baby kinkajou, and Tom brought home a month-old black leopard, whose fickle mother had deserted her last cub, and couldn't be trusted with this one.

He had finished work on the bungalow love nest, after painting the front door five times in different colours, and the chemist and his finicky bride got married. Tom was invited to the wedding, but he couldn't go, because he had nothing to wear. He was on another job anyway, helping a man to build a garage.

Em had wanted to stand outside the church with the other village women who had not been invited, and say, 'Isn't she lovely?' (or worse things) as the spliced couple came out. But Mrs Potter was one of the guests, and so Em had to go up to Orchards to look after her three children.

Liza was doing house calls with Alec Harvey. Michael was off with the Mismos, who had gone to a relation in the Isle of Wight, so that no one would know they had not been invited to the wedding.

Carrie's friend Lester came over to help her with Irma, the leopard cub.

He arrived, as he often did, unexpectedly, and by a surprise route. Carrie was in her bedroom with Irma in a play pen lent by Mrs Potter (who was off babies for good, after little Jocelyn), asleep on a blanket over a hot water bottle. Charlie leaned his chin on the top rail and whined, and the cats were affronted, stalking about on shelves and the top of the cupboard.

Carrie was working on her *Book of Horses*. John had galloped at thirty-three miles an hour yesterday, timed by the laundry man, driving along the road by a big grass field. Carrie was writing a poem about it.

'Thirty-three miles an hour!
O the speed, and O the power.
John's flying hoofs are drum beats on the turf.
His neck and shoulders surge and plunge like surf.
Away! Away! The wind roars in my ears.
Is it the wind – or joy that brings the tears?'

Crash! Thump! The trapdoor to the attic banged down, and Lester landed lightly as a cat in the passage outside Carrie's door.

'How did you get in?' Carrie had learned not to be scared by his sudden appearances.

'Through the skylight. Guess what I found in the attic.'

Carrie thought she and Em and Michael had explored all the abondoned relics of the family who once lived here, but Lester could always find something different.

He held out his closed fist. 'I was crawling under that low beam. It was between the floor boards.'

He opened his hand and showed her a chain with a silver locket in the shape of a heart.

'It doesn't open.'

Carrie tried, but there was no catch, or else the locket was stuck tight with age. It was blackened and tarnished, but you could make out the engraved letters, and a date: C.F. 1808.

'My own initials.' Carrie looked at Lester. 'I wonder who—?'

'You have been here before.' Lester put the chain over her head, and she tucked the silver heart inside her shirt. It was cold on her skin.

'Do you think that was why – when I first saw this house ...' When Carrie first saw World's End, the house

36

and the dusty great barn and the cobwebbed stable, redolent of horse, had called to her like an old friend.

'How's Irma?' Lester dropped the subject abruptly, as he often did when you got close to mysterious truths.

The black cub, faintly spotted with her future markings, was yawning and stretching in the play pen. She lay on her back with her paws in the air, opened her kitten mouth in a mewing cry, then rolled over and nuzzled into the blanket searching.

'You want your Mum.' Carrie bent over and lifted her out. 'But you'll have to make do with me.' She washed the cub over with a piece of damp towel, to imitate her faithless mother's tongue. 'Abandoned,' she said, 'like that baby the vicar found in a shopping bag in the church porch. I'd never do that to you, Irma.'

'You might if you were a wild animal in captivity.' Lester got inside the play pen and squatted there, rattling the bars like a caged gorilla. 'If you couldn't find a proper den, and hunt for bedding and stuff in your own natural way, you wouldn't be ready to be a mother.'

'I never shall be,' Carrie said. Em was going to have ten babies. Carrie was going to stay with animals.

'Want to know something?' Lester licked the paint of Mrs Potter's play pen to see if he would get lead poisoning. 'There's a circus over at Wareham.'

'Are you going?'

'I don't want to. But I want to. The animals – it's like when people were in the stocks, or executed on Tower Hill. Most of the crowd were there to jeer, but a few were there for sympathy.'

'I'll come with you,' Carrie said. 'Oh – but I can't leave Irma. I wonder—'

A dog barked somewhere, quite far off. Perpetua, asleep on Carrie's bed, lifted her head and raised her tattered ears. Charlie ran out of the room with the silly womanish yelp he used when he was excited, and his nails skittered down the uncarpeted stairs.

The dog barked again, a deep, two-syllable bark, *bassoprofundo*, Rodge called it. Wendy hardly ever barked, but he had taught her to speak a kind of Thank You when he was out with her helping the guide dog fund.

'Wendy.'

Lester got out of the play pen. Carrie put Irma back into it and followed him downstairs.

Out in the lane, they saw nothing. Charlie had disappeared. They called, and Rodge's voice answered, faint and muffled.

'He's in the wood.'

They ran round the corner. The lane was empty under the tunnel of greening branches.

'Where are you?'

'If I knew,' his voice was nearer, 'I wouldn't be here. Wendy won't move. I – ouch!'

They plunged into the wood, and searched through the undergrowth in the direction of his voice. Ducking under a fallen tree, they found him sitting on the ground with his jacket torn, holding his head. He was hemmed in by bracken and bramble bushes. In front of him, Charlie and Wendy sat by the fallen tree into which he had just crashed.

'Now I know why she couldn't go a – go a – ' he felt for the top of his head to see if it was still there. 'Ahead.'

'Taking a short cut?' Lester asked.

'No fear. Blind men don't go into woods. I was on the side of the road, and a car came by too fast, too near.'

'Drunken revellers from the chemist's wedding,' Lester said.

'I jum-jumped away.' Rodge's nervous mouth twitched. His hands were shaking. 'I fell in the ditch and lost hold of Wendy. I got up and she came to me, but I must have gone the wrong way. I was – I was in the trees. We got

38

stuck in the brambles, and then Wendy wouldn't move. "Speak," I told her. So she spo-spo-spoke.'

At home, Carrie bathed the lumpy bruise with vinegar and bicarbonate of soda, and Lester made hot sweet tea in case of shock. Rodge was still a bit shaky, so Lester sloshed into the tea a swig of the brandy Mr Mismo had given them for emergencies, like birthdays, or dying goldfish.

'Better.' Rodge put down the cup, and patted his beard with a hand that was steadier. 'You two go and ride, or something. Wendy and I will take care of Irma. I've got a lot of work to do.' Rodge had to work much harder than the other teachers, because his fingers had to learn the music and songs in Braille before he could teach them.

'Are you sure you're all right, Rodge?' Carrie worried. He looked frail, sitting there with the darkening bruise over one eye, and the strong, quiet dog at his feet.

'Go away and don't ba-ba-baby me,' he said, quite irritably, so they went.

eight

Tightening her girth in the stable, Carrie stopped, and John took the opportunity to blow himself out with air again.

'I haven't got any money,' she called to Lester, who was already on Peter in the yard, riding bareback with a halter, the way he liked to ride, the way Peter liked to be ridden, but only by Lester.

'I know how we can get in free,' he said.

Lester's mother pretended to pull her hair out in despairing grey handfuls, because he added on his fingers, and got bad marks at school, but he knew all the things in life worth knowing.

He knew all the people worth knowing too. He knew a man in Wareham, who had a boatyard by the river near the field where the circus had pitched its tents and caravans. The man moved out a punt and two skiffs, and let them tie John and Peter at one end of the long shed where his boats had been stored for the winter.

It was almost time for the circus to start. A straggle of people were buying tickets from a woman in a booth. Lester and Carrie bent double to creep under her window, and stood by the opening of the tent to see if there was a chance to slip in.

Inside, the tiers of seats were only half full. Children shouted and fidgeted, and clattered up and down the wooden tiers and got slapped at. An elderly clown, big round tears painted on his white cheeks and a huge crimson mouth turned down to his chin at the corners, hopped round the barrier of the ring in a ludicrous dance. No one looked at him. Boys with pimples and dirty white caps carried round trays of popcorn and candy floss, chanting mournfully, '*Get* your popcorn ee-yer!'

The band was playing clash, tootle and oompah, but in spite of the music and the glaring lights and the rainbow swags of the tent roof, it was a fairly depressing scene.

The man who was taking the tickets had a villainous scar down one side of his face, and a heavy sharp ring that looked like a weapon.

When two teachers shepherded a bunch of labelled children into the tent, Lester and Carrie joined the end of the line. The man grabbed one of them in each hand, and spun them out again.

'I been watching you,' he said.

Lester did not bother to pretend that he was with the schoolchildren. He respected a man who couldn't be fooled. The man respected Lester for trying. They winked at each other, and Lester took Carrie round to the back of the tent, where the performers were gathering for the opening parade.

A coach drawn by six Shetland ponies, with a stonefaced Cinderella inside smoking and reading a magazine. Three elephants, shifting their massive feet, brushing the ground with their trunks. Spangled acrobats with splits in the seams of their tights. Plumed Liberty horses. A man in white tie and tails with an armfull of small, excited dogs. A young man and a girl standing on a grey percheron rosinback. Behind them, a woman with frizzed hair and gold teeth, sitting sideways on another broad grey. At the back of the procession, half a dozen clowns were getting themselves underneath a dragon outfit made of cardboard and canvas.

The band went ta-ra-ra-*ra*! Cinderella threw out the cigarette and put the magazine under her seat. Her grumpy dwarf coachman slapped the reins, and the ponies moved forward to the *oom*-pa-pa-*pa*-pa.

The man with the dogs threw them on to the barrier to run round and round, yelping and jumping over each other and turning somersaults. They were dressed in tutus or baggy trousers, with little fancy hats held on by elastic. The hat of a black and white terrier had slipped over his eye, but he went on running and turning somersaults.

The Liberty horses came in on their hind legs, front hoofs waving desperately to keep their balance, necks arched and jaws forced open by tight bearing reins. A man with a goad, its spike disguised by ribbons, jabbed it here and there, and the elephants plodded forward in their sagging skin. The young man on the percheron hoisted the girl on to his shoulders. The woman on the horse behind blew kisses from her gold teeth. The clown inside the dragon's head puffed fire out of its jaws with a blow lamp. Lester and Carrie slipped under the painted canvas scales, and trotted into the tent inside its tail.

Just before it got into the ring, they ducked out, and crawled round under the tiers of benches. The parade passed out on the other side, and a man on a trapeze swung out from the roof, with the glaring spotlight on him. While everyone was gazing upwards with their mouths open and their stomachs turning over each time the trapeze artist turned over, Lester and Carrie walked casually up the steps, and sat down on a bench near the front.

It was not a very good circus. It toured the country with its train of animals, putting on second rate shows for people who dragged along the kiddies because it reminded them of their lost youth.

Lester and Carrie sat glumly, with their elbows on their knees and their chins in their hands, saying, 'Some liberty' loudly enough for the trainer of the overflexed Liberty horses to hear; and, 'He pricks it with a pin,' when the talking horse nodded or shook its head; and, 'I hope they kill him,' when the brave White Hunter was in the cage with the mangy, cowed lions.

When the elephants came in, Carrie glanced at Lester.

He was clutching the bench, knuckles white, his mouth set into a hard line in his thin brown face, his eyes blank, looking back into another life. He had once been a circus elephant, humiliated and beaten, shot when he rebelled. He had told Carrie that, and she believed it.

'They laughed at me,' he had told her, his face pale with memory, his dark eyes haunted. 'People in the crowd laughed at me, because I couldn't do the tricks.'

A blare of trumpets. The crowd clapped and laughed as the great elephants shambled into the ring like conquered heroes. Behind each huge grey head with its tiny sad eye, rode a girl in a leopardskin bikini, with a wig and false eyelashes. Ugly and grinning, with blue goose pimples on their legs, the girls hung on by the head harness while the elephants did embarrassing, unelephantine things like crawling, rolling over, and propping their front feet on each other's backs.

A drum roll. The girls jumped down and took a strutting bow, as if they had done something clever. Two of the elephants stood on the front of their heads, with their ponderous back legs waving meekly in the air. The third was slow getting his heavy back feet up, and the man with the ribboned goad poked him in the stomach.

Lester uttered a groan, and doubled over, clutching himself as if he was ill.

'What's the matter, sonny?' A motherly woman leaned over and put her hand on his arm. 'Too much candy floss?'

'It's the elephants,' Carrie said.

'Aren't they funny, the dear clumsy things,' the woman maundered, 'and to think it's all done by kindness.'

Lester groaned again, and Carrie felt his wrenching hurt within herself.

'If you're going to throw up,' the motherly woman passed him a paper bag full of eggshells and apple cores, 'you can do it in there.'

*   *   *

The bareback family was called The Rosinellas.

The girl and the young man did most of the riding and balancing and jumping on and off the horses, while the mother stood in the middle with a whip, and the patient percherons cantered round and round, long manes flopping to the rocking horse rhythm.

The second horse, who looked much older, began to blow and sweat while the front one was still quite fresh. He fell back a pace or two, and the young man almost missed a jump.

Balancing in his soft shoes on the broad, moving back, he growled something to the horse. He had a face like a snake, slant eyes, high cheeks between oily sideburns.

The girl stood on her hands on the front horse. The young man stood on his. As he dropped his feet on to the rump in a back flip, the grey horse half stumbled. The rider slipped, recovered himself, stood upright with his arms wide, and jumped down to the sawdust.

Running across the ring to vault on again as the horse cantered round, he turned his glossy head and muttered, 'Use the whip on him, Ma.'

The mother flicked the long whip behind the old horse, but she didn't touch him.

It was not a very good act. The boy was quick and agile, but he was out of temper with the horse. The small dark girl was graceful and pretty, but she seemed nervous. Towards the end, she jumped down and took the whip, and Ma Rosinella did a few cautious jumps and feats of balance on the second horse, which was blowing quite hard by now, and dropping his head.

When the mother came down from a handstand, and posed for thin applause, with her hands out and her frizzed head flung back, she was puffing too. She was a bit past it, like the horse.

*   *   *

The man in white tie and tails came in with the dogs: terriers, poodles, mongrels. They wore bonnets and shawls and pushed each other in prams. They jumped through hoops. They jumped through fire. They climbed a ladder and dived into a small tank of water. They chased the elderly clown round the ring, nipping at his pantaloons.

The audience roared. Behind Lester and Carrie, a jovial father and two children howled with laughter. When the black and white terrier stood on one fore leg on the man's outstretched hand, with its back legs in the air and its stump tail wagging, they split their sides.

'Tell them, Carrie,' Lester said grimly, and she turned round.

'Don't encourage them to laugh,' she found herself saying. 'It's cruel.'

'Oh get away,' the father said. 'He loves it.'

'Don't you know how he's trained?'

The man in tails was strutting round the ring with the terrier still upended on the palm of his hand, while the audience clapped and hooted.

'Another man takes the dog and beats him up and hangs him by one hind leg from a hook in the ceiling,' Carrie said. 'When he's in agony, this man comes in and puts his hand under a front paw to take the strain, and he pets the dog and feeds him. That's how he learns to stand on one paw – as relief from torture.'

The children stared. The father winced. 'But he's wagging his tail,' he said doubtfully.

'If you beat your head against a wall,' Lester said loudly, without turning round, 'it feels lovely when you stop.'

'Go away,' said the jovial father unhappily. 'We were having fun, but you've upset me proper.'

nine

Carrie and Lester went out and wandered round the sideshows. They could not pay to go into any of them, so they stood outside and listened to the showmen raving about the Smallest Lady on Earth and the Man-Eating Ape, and the Two-headed Baby, and the Rubber Lady, and the Blood-sweating Hippopotamus.

The only tent that wasn't pegged down too tightly for them to crawl under was the Man-Eating Ape.

The man-eater sat mournfully in a dark cage, picking through peanut shells and fruit skins. He was not much bigger than Joey, the woolly monkey who had lived at World's End for a while. Carrie tried to talk to him in the chirruping monkey chatter that had worked with Joey, but the ape turned his humped back and wouldn't answer.

Out in the field among the crowd who were coming out of the circus tent, Carrie and Lester turned out their pockets and the lining of Carrie's jacket, which collected what fell through her pockets, and found they had enough for one sideshow between them.

Roundabout, Dodgems, Switchback, Jet Rocket to the Moon, where girls were whirled upside down, shrieking and all the change fell out of a man's pocket?

'Let's do something where we can win a prize,' Carrie said, as she and Lester knelt to pick up the man's money. 'A clock, or a dish, something we can take home. A toy for Michael.'

'Michael doesn't play with toys,' Lester said.

'Only because he never has any.'

They gave the man his money as he staggered off the Jet Rocket, his face marbled green and white, and he rewarded them with a coin. Now they had enough for two tries to win something.

Lester went round the shooting gallery and the coconut shy and the Roll-a-Ball, judging the prizes with the tight, careful mouth his mother made at the supermarket.

He came to rest at the hoopla. There it was. In the middle of the circular stall, farthest away from wherever you might throw.

A transistor radio.

Apart from the fact that it was set into the stomach of a repulsive purple rabbit, with two plastic teeth smirking between nylon whiskers, it was just what World's End needed. There was no electricity to plug anything in. They had always wanted a transistor, but there were always more important things to buy if anyone ever had any extra cash.

Someone else wanted the purple rabbit radio too. A watery young man with no chin or eyelashes was desperately casting hoops at it.

His girl friend stood cynically by. 'Turn it in, Harold,' she said. 'You'll never get it in a million years.'

'Who says?' He fished out money for another go. 'What Harold Snelling wants, Harold Snelling gets.'

'Har, har,' said the girl.

'Watch this.' The next hoop fell over the rabbit's ear.

'It has to be right over the whole thing to win,' Carrie said helpfully.

'I know.' He threw again, on to the other ear.

'Good try, sir,' Lester said, in the sporting voice he used for village cricket matches.

'Next one will do it.' The young man sucked his bottom teeth into his receding chin, took aim, flung, missed. The bored hoopla man picked up the ring on his stick like a robot.

'Har blooming har,' said the girl, and started to walk away.

'Clarisse!' The young man went after her with his desperate pink eyes. 'Where are you going?'

'To see the freaks. Not that they'll be any change from you.'

'But you wanted the tranny!'

'Some hope.' Her cynical bottom disappeared into the tent of the Two-headed Baby.

Lester had paid one of the coins. He gave the three rings to Carrie. 'You go first.'

'I'll mess it up.'

'Throw it high so it drops down over the ears.'

'It's impossible.' The young man could not help coming back to the rabbit. 'It's a cheat.'

Without a word the robot man took a ring and passed it easily over the rabbit.

Carrie threw. Her rings went all over the place, nowhere near where she was aiming. Her last one almost fell over a card with a hideous clown brooch on it.

'Bad luck,' Harold Snelling said generously, because Carrie was worse than him.

'I wouldn't want that anyway.'

But the brooch reminded her of the silver pendant. As Lester threw, with one eye shut like a sharpshooter, Carrie put her hand inside the old denim shirt of Tom's she was wearing, and held the little flat heart.

Lester's first ring was near. The second ring nearer. The third ring sailed high, hesitated, and dropped right over the tips of the rabbit's ears, wiggled down the purple body and came neatly to rest without touching the squatting paws.

'You could knock me down.' The watery young man looked as if he were going to flow tearfully into the ground.

The hoopla man never moved a muscle. He handed over the rabbit, and turned away to the other side of the stall, as if people won a transistor every day of the week. Perhaps it didn't work.

Carrie let go of the silver heart, and turned on the radio. It worked beautifully.

'We can always take it out, and give the rabbit to Irma to play with,' Lester said. No question of his taking his prize to his own home. He spent all his spare time at World's End anyway.

They walked off, making music among the straggling crowds on the sour, trodden grass between the sideshows.

'I say there.' The young man panted after them. 'I say, would you sell me that tranny?'

'Sell?' Carrie stopped. She had thought only of the transistor. Now she thought of the red flour crock with Michael's label: 'SAVVING WORLD END'.

'For my dolly bird.'

'You could buy her another.' Lester had the rabbit under his arm, feet one side, whiskers the other, music coming out of his armpit.

'Not like that one. Never seen one like it, and she took a fancy for it.' He looked back towards the two-headed baby tent, and gabbled, 'She thinks I'm no good at anything, see? But if she thought I'd won the rabbit – oops, here she comes.' The girl came out of the tent and mooched towards them.

'I'll give you twenty pounds for it,' the young man said desperately.

'Twenty pounds!' Carrie didn't think the radio was worth half that.

'Done,' Lester said crisply.

'It's a deal.' The young man pulled out a wad of notes that made their eyes bulge, licked a finger and counted them out, looking nervously over his shoulder.

Lester gave him the rabbit radio, just as the girl came up, with a grating whine, 'Two-headed baby, what a cheat.

It was three inches high and pickled in a glass jar.'

'Look what I won for you, Clarisse.' Harold Snelling held out the rabbit.

'Well, you could knock me down.' She sauntered off, without even touching the rabbit.

ten

Lester and Carrie went behind a dynamo lorry and took off their shoes. They divided some notes, in each shoe under the foot, in case of robbery, or one of them losing a leg in an accident. The rest went into the aerated match box which Lester carried with him as an ambulance for wounded insects.

On the way to get John and Peter, and ride home with the marvellous news, which burned the soles of their feet at every step, they walked through the tent where the horse lines were.

Carrie wanted to go up to each tethered horse, but the man who trained the Liberty horses recognized her, and chased her away with a broom.

She went behind some bales of hay. On the other side, the two big great percherons were tied in stalls, with a swinging pole between them.

Lester went to talk to the younger one, who had led the act with the nervous girl on his back. Carrie went up to the older horse. He had fading dapples on the strong muscle of his shoulder, and on his huge round quarters. He dropped his heavy head into her hand. His long white forelock fell into his blue eyes, and she stood on tiptoe to put it back behind his ears.

'You like His Lordship, dear?' Ma Rosinella was sitting on a bale of straw, with her frizzy hair in small rollers to make it frizzier, picking her gold teeth with a match.

'He's beautiful.' Carrie would have said that about any horse, but the grey percheron, with his massive chest and crested neck, did have a special beauty in his proud, controlled strength.

'He's old, poor lamb. Past it really, I don't know.'

'Put a sock in it, Ma.' The oily son had been oiling tack. He came up, cleaning the long nails of one hand with the nails of the other. 'Lazy brute is good for two more seasons at least, if you'd do your job and not let him dope off.'

'I'll not take the whip to him,' the mother said. 'Fifteen years he's worked for us, and just because your Dad's not here any more, I'll not let you abuse him.'

Carrie laid her cheek against the hoary muzzle of the horse, but she was listening. So was Lester.

'It's our living, Ma.'

'Get another horse. You've weeks before our next booking.'

'Put a sock in it.'

When he had gone away, Carrie said to Ma Rosinella, 'You're right. The horse is too old. He didn't stumble on purpose. It's because, when they get old, they get a bit anaemic, you see, and that will cause some nerve and muscle weakness, so they may drop a foot sometimes, if they place it wrong.'

'Yes,' the mother said, getting that glazed look that came over even the most intelligent faces when Carrie launched into horse lectures. 'But my son is stubborn. He won't get a new horse, because he's no good at training them, see. Not like his poor Dad. Do anything with a horse, his Dad could. He had His Lordship from a colt. I'd like to pension the old fellow off, if I knew somewhere.'

'Tell her, Carrie,' Lester said, and Carrie said quickly, 'There's World's End.'

'What's that, a pub?'

'It was. Now it's where we live. There would be lots of room for—' She couldn't bring herself to say 'His Lordship' – 'this good old horse.'

'My son would kill me.'

'Don't tell him. Say some stupid kids – me and Lester, if

52

you like – untied the halter rope, and he got away.'

'He'll find him.'

'We'll hide him.' Lester came out of the stall towards her, his lively, shining eyes reflecting the challenge of adventure. 'Trust us.'

'Perhaps I do,' Ma Rosinella said in surprise, 'though I never did trust my own boy when he was your age. Or now, come to that. But it's no good, my dears. You couldn't afford it.'

'The spring grass is coming in.' Carrie left the horse to stand in front of her too, hugging her growing excitement. 'It wouldn't cost much to keep him, and we – oh. Oh, I see.' She looked down at her moneyed feet, and shuffled her toe in a wisp of hay. 'You want us to buy the horse.'

'Have to, my dear. I'm in trouble with the feed man here. My son doesn't know. He gave me the money for the bill, and I gave it to a girl whose husband ran out on her. Tumblers, they are. But he tumbled too far, and broke up the act. That's worse than breaking up the marriage.'

'How much?'

'Well – eighteen quid would clear my debts. Twenty-two, if I'm to pay back a loan from my son's wife, before he finds out the poor girl lent it me. So there you are. It's back on the road for His poor old Lordship.'

The trouble with Carrie was that whenever she took in any money, it usually went out again before it got to the red crock.

She and Lester looked at each other, without speaking or moving their faces.

The look said, *The twenty pounds is for the World's End fund.*

But here is a horse.

Think of taking home all that money.

Think of taking home this lovely old horse, and turning him into the hill field . . .

'Been on the go since before Christmas,' Ma Rosinella said, as if she had intercepted the look, and de-coded it. 'He's not been turned out to graze for months. If you could only raise twenty-two pounds. Make it twenty—'

'Done.' Carrie and Lester sat down and began to take off their shoes. 'It's a deal.'

eleven

As soon as the percheron was officially theirs, they changed his name to Roy.

'Why Roy?' Ma Rosinella tucked the notes into the top of her spangled costume.

'Because he is the kind of horse who used to carry kings.' Carrie could imagine the big grey horse in all the trappings of monarchy, gold saddle cloth and gorgeous jingling bridle, stepping proudly under the royal banner.

'Well, suit yourself. It takes all kinds. As long as you can get the old fellow away without trouble. No,' she said, as Lester looked left and right with his conspirator's face, and bent to her ear. 'Don't tell me how you're going to do it. Then I won't know.'

'You don't need to.' Lester went over to the other ear, and whispered through the metal rollers. 'But you must all go out after the evening show. Go out to supper. Tell your son it's your birthday. He doesn't sound as if he would remember the date.'

He and Carrie went back to the boatyard. When John heard Carrie's feet on the gravel of the yard, he let out a call that echoed through the big shed.

She held him and Peter outside, while Lester helped his friend to put back the punt and the two skiffs. They took the horses down to the river to drink, and let them graze in the water meadow. Lester and Carrie sat in an old boat turned on its side, and watched the light go out of the river, and the opposite bank grow dim, and disappear.

When they had laid their plans for the rescue of Roy, they talked about food, and what they would be eating if they had blown the whole of the rabbit radio money on a dinner at Mabel's Table, the best hostelry in Wareham.

It began to rain. But this was good, because the side-shows would be closed early after the circus. They moved the horses along the riverbank, nearer to the showground.

They saw the lights of the big top go out. The music, which was only a beat of drums and brass from here, was gone. One by one, the roundabout, the flying chairs, the Jet Rocket stopped. The lights dimmed, and the glow of the circus left the sky. The throbbing dynamo was still.

Lester waited with the horses under the bridge which took the road over the river, while Carrie stood near the gate to watch the cars drive out.

In a red car was the oily son driving, his wife with her hair down and a child on her lap, and Ma Rosinella in the back seat, glancing back with sad eyes through the rear window, as if she were saying a secret farewell to the grey horse.

Carrie ran back to Lester under the bridge.

'They've gone.'

'You start off for home.' His low voice was hollow under the stone arch. 'Don't wait for me. If I'm caught, you mustn't be involved.'

'Thanks—'

'For nothing. If they get me, you must be free to rescue Roy.'

Carrie got on John, and Lester handed her up Peter's halter rope. Crossing the bridge among the evening traffic, with two horses who were restless from waiting, was no picnic. Some cars slowed, others zipped past too close. Twice Peter pulled back, and Carrie almost let go of the rope. The rest of the time, he pushed too close to John, crushing Carrie's leg, and making John put back his ears and nip at him. When John nipped, Peter nipped back. Once he nipped Carrie's knee. In pain, she whacked him on the nose, and he shied away, close to the parapet. A car hooted, and Carrie almost lost Peter again.

Across the bridge, she turned on to the path that wound through open fields, and the horses relaxed, and trotted quietly, snorting into the dark. The rain had stopped, and Carrie would have enjoyed the silent, mysterious ride through the wet grass, but her chest was tight with excitement, and anxiety for Lester.

At the end of the soft track, she turned alongside a hedge, where unseen birds stirred with a whispered cheep. She dropped down through the gap on to the road, leaning back almost out of the saddle to lead Peter behind her.

They clattered like smugglers through a small village, past dark cottages where people slept with all the windows shut. It was like the smuggling poem:

Five and twenty ponies, trotting through the dark.
Brandy for the parson, baccy for the clerk.
Laces for a lady, letters for a spy.
So watch the wall, my darling, while the gentlemen go by.

Some way beyond the village, Carrie stopped to listen. If Lester's plan worked right, and he had got the big horse out of the tent, and squeezed him through the narrow gate in the dark corner of the field, he should be on the road by now.

Carrie's ears were good. She could hear things that people said about her three rooms away with all the doors shut. She could hear John tearing grass on a summer night, half way up the long hill field.

Now she could hear nothing. But John and Peter raised their heads with their ears strained forward, and Peter, who had an undying curiosity about strange horses, whinnied.

A deep answering whinny, back along the road. The grey shape of Roy loomed like a ghost out of the darkness, before Carrie heard his hoofs. Lester had tied bits of sacking round his feet. He looked like one of the elephants.

'But John and Peter heard him quite far away,' Carrie said.

'It's like when you put your ear to the railway line.' Lester's father had spanked him with a fly whisk for doing this. 'They felt the vibrations on the ground.'

Roy was so broad that Lester's legs astride him stuck out at right angles. He had been tied with a leather collar in the tent, so Lester was riding him in John's rope halter, let out on a loose knot, but still too tight for his large head.

'What's he like?' Carrie's eyes devoured the huge grey horse, with his soft blue eyes and his long silver mane flowing like water over his crested neck.

'Dreamy. You have to walk or canter, because he's been taught not to trot. Have a go.'

Lester slipped off, and hoisted Carrie up on to the broad grey back. Roy was over seventeen hands high. It felt like a skyscraper. She looked over a hedge she had never seen over before, into the bland white face of a ruminating Hereford cow.

There was no more hard road, so Lester took the sacks off Roy's feet, and buried them among leaves, to leave no clues. He got on Peter and led John, trotting down a long cart track which followed the side of the wood.

Not being able to use her legs, because they were stuck out sideways, Carrie said, 'Canter,' and Roy moved into the slowest, smoothest canter she had ever sat on.

John cantered 'as if he had five legs,' Mr Mismo said, but Carrie had got used to his rolling stride. Peter cantered rather high, always competing to go faster. Oliver's short legs cantered choppy and quick. Alec Harvey's thoroughbred, which he let Carrie ride sometimes, never went slower than a gallop with her. The donkey Leonora never went faster than a jog. Carrie had never known a canter like this, the broad back level, the legs moving supple and slow, like thick cream.

But her own legs were soon in agony. She lifted the right one over and sat sideways, holding on to Roy's mane, and blowing kisses to the applause of an imaginary crowd.

'When we get home,' she called to Lester's dark head, bobbing in front of her, 'I'm going to ride him standing up.'

'We're not going to take him home. Yet. Ma Rosinella's son has seen us, don't forget. If he does come out this way looking, and sees one of us, he might get an idea in that greasy head.'

They did not turn up the slope at the edge of the wood to come through the top gate of their own field. After a brief, fierce battle with John and Peter, who knew the way home, Lester managed to turn them across the tussocky field that dropped down to the brook on the other side of their hill. They crossed the hump-backed bridge on the Beddington road, and stopped by the gate of Mr Mosmo's small calf pasture that was farthest from his farm.

Carrie slid off Roy, jarring her knee joints from the height of the jump, and took him through the gate. He had scraped a large patch of skin off one hip squeezing through the narrow gate of the circus field, so he tucked it coyly away from the gatepost, like an overgrown hula-hula dancer. Carrie pulled off the tight halter with a struggle, and turned him loose.

She and Lester watched over the gate. Roy walked round and round with his nose down, until he found the choice, the perfect spot to roll. He pawed at the ground, turned round like a dog making a bed, sagged, thought better of it, turned round again, sagged, and finally flopped down with the thump of a bomb dropping.

He rolled ecstatically, waving his silly big feet in the air, rubbing his head and neck so violently on the ground, to get rid of the smell and feel of the circus. He was too broad to roll over, so after he had squirmed on one side, he got up and went down on the other – thump! They must have heard him two miles away.

He got up, shook, and then the ghostly grey shape wandered off into the darkness.

They heard him tearing at the grass like a starving castaway.

'What shall we tell Mr Mismo?'

'I'll think of something tomorrow.' Lester yawned, and neck-reined Peter towards the bridge. 'I've done enough brilliant thinking for one night.'

twelve

After stopping at Mr Mismo's farm to check Pygmalia, they put John and Peter in the stable with an enormous feed. Oliver stood on his back legs and hung his front hoofs over his half door, so they gave him a handful of bran and cracked maize. He shared it with Lucy, the Nubian goat who slept with him.

Carrie and Lester ran for the house, their stomachs turning over as they got near food. Rodge was giving Irma a bottle, and everyone was home from their various jobs.

Nobody said, 'Where have you *been*?' It wasn't that kind of family. Tom said, 'Have you had supper?' Em said, 'We ate all the stew.' Liza began to fry bacon to make the World's Biggest Sandwich, her speciality of bacon and tomato and pickles and mustard and mayonnaise and chopped onion, with an egg fried just hard enough to keep it from spurting when you bit into the bread.

'How was the ride?' Rodge asked.

'Marvellous.'

'You must have been half way to London.' Rodge put down Irma's empty bottle, and felt the raised figures on his Braille watch. The leopard cub rolled on to her back, sleepily dribbling milk, her soft round stomach distended.

'We rode over to the other side of Wareham,' Carrie said. True.

'Is it that far?'

'We followed the river for miles, to try to find its source.' Carrie invariably spoiled either truth or lies by embroidering them a bit too far to be believed.

'There's a circus at Wareham.' Em sat opposite her and stared.

'Is there?' Slumped at the round table, waiting for food, Carrie closed her eyes against the stare, and fell into a half doze behind her hair, her fingers playing with the silver heart round her neck.

Em, who always noticed what people wore, leaned across the table. 'Where did you get that?'

Carrie pulled out the locket and showed it to her. 'It was in the attic.'

'C.F.,' Em read. 'What's in it?'

'It doesn't open. But it's the same initials as me. It proves I was here before. Ages ago, in the days when they went everywhere on horses. I dressed up as a boy, I expect, and went to war on a charger.'

'You would,' Em said. 'Though it would serve you right if you were one of those soppy girls in long frilly bloomers, fainting at mice. Here, give me the locket. I'll polish it for you.'

'No.' Carrie put it back inside her shirt. She wasn't ever going to take it off. They could bury her in it. 'I like it like this. It brought us luck today.'

'We could do with a bit of that.' Tom's eyes went up to the hanging red crock. 'I got a letter from Uncle Rudolf. He's coming down soon, to find a surveyor to look at the land.'

'What luck?' Em asked. 'Did you win something at the circus?'

'I didn't say we went there.'

'But did you?'

'No.' Carrie looked at Lester. 'I mean – we can't tell you. Yet.'

'Come on,' Tom said. 'You know we said when there were no grown-ups here, we wouldn't have secrets from each other.'

'Rodge is a grown-up.'

'He doesn't count.'

62

'Ta,' said Rodge. 'Even if that was meant as an insult, I take it as a compliment.'

'It's better for you all not to know,' Lester said.

If Ma Rosinella's son did come round asking awkward questions, Tom and Em and Liza could get rid of him more efficiently, if they genuinely didn't know about Roy.

'Oh Lord,' Tom groaned. 'You two have stolen a horse again.'

'No,' Carrie and Lester said together. That was the genuine truth, since they had paid for Roy.

Liza gave them each a giant sandwich, which would need the jaws of a whale to get round it, and they took the plates to bed, with cocoa in the thick pottery beakers Michael had made. They had started life as mugs, but the handles had dropped off the first time they were used.

Tomorrow was Sunday, so Lester was staying the night. He slept in the little room downstairs that had once been the Snug at the back of the Public Bar. The walls were patchy and peeling, so Lester had papered them with pages torn from an obsolete timetable given him by his father, who worked for the railway. When Lester could not sleep, because ideas buzzed in his head and he could not wait for the promise of tomorrow, he lit a candle, and figured out how he could have got from Polperro to Stirling in the shortest time in 1902.

As Carrie was finishing her sandwich, Rodge and Wendy came in to say goodnight.

Rodge knew his way about so well that Wendy never had to lead him inside the house. She pushed open the door with her thick, pinky-brown nose, and jumped on to Carrie's legs to clean up crumbs from the blanket.

Rodge came in behind her. He put out a hand to feel the foot of the bed, then moved cautiously along the rug, feeling with his foot for sleeping cats or puppies.

'Ouch.' He stubbed his toe on Carrie's horse book on the floor. 'Goodnight.' He bent to kiss her. His beard was soft, like kissing a cat, and smelled of soap.

'Do you always kiss goodnight, because your mother used to do it to you?' Carrie asked.

'No,' Rodge said. 'It's because she didn't.'

'Why not?'

'Because I couldn't see, she wanted to make me super tough, and not dependent.'

'Well, she failed miserably,' Carrie said.

'I'm not dependent,' Rodge said quickly.

'Except on Wendy.'

'Oh, well.'

Although she was tired, Carrie still felt like a balloon, blown up too tight with excitement not told.

She had to say, 'I'll tell you a secret.'

She told him about Roy. Rodge sat on the bed with his hands dug into Wendy's golden coat, and kept his eyes on Carrie's face, as if he was hearing through them.

'I can't wait to see the horse,' he said.

'But if Ma Rosinella's son comes here, can you swear you have never set eyes on Roy?'

'Of course.' Rodge got up, felt for Wendy, and pulled her off the bed. 'Because I won't have.'

After Rodge had gone, Carrie rode John up to the Star, where there were all the horses from all the years since men and horses began to keep company together.

Favourites waited for friends on earth to die, and come to fetch them. Famous horses of history strolled about on the endless pastures that were always sweet with spring grass, and told tall tales of their past to anyone who would listen.

That night, when John came to Carrie's bedroom window, snorting gently and pawing the air, he had Roy with him. They bounded up through the night sky, Roy moving alongside with his effortless big-footed canter. Clouds curled damp about Carrie's face, and streamed her hair down her back. Then they broke through into the clean cold sky, and threaded their way between lesser stars to the one where the horses were.

Carrie and John were well known, but several horses looked up curiously as Roy ambled on to the springy turf and stood out well, hocks back, head and tail high, for admiration. He was used to the crowds, so he did not mind being stared at.

'Ho, ho, what's this?' Alexander's big black charger Bucephalus came up, stepping arrogantly.

Roy explained that he was from the circus, just retired.

'Another barnstormer.' No one but a war horse was any good in the opinion of Bucephalus. 'This place is crawling with 'em. Liberty horses. Not an idea in their fool heads, because they've been trained like machines. Dancing horses. La-di-da – my dear, my arabesque!' He minced a few steps. 'Trick horses like that old fake Clever Hans – whoops – Hallo, Hans.' He took a kick from the rear from the angry trick horse. 'I didn't know you were there.'

'Say fake again, and I'll kick your lying teeth in.'

'Well, but some doctors did prove you were obeying signals instead of actually counting.' Bucephalus jumped a hedge and stayed on the other side. Jumping was about the only thing Clever Hans couldn't do.

'Those doctors were quacks. Here, Little L!' Hans raised his head and neighed towards the low hills which rolled towards the blue distance, dotted with grazing horses. 'Come and meet one of us!'

A small, short-backed horse with a tiny head and perky ears came galloping, splashed through a stream, and trotted up to inspect Roy with professional interest.

He was the Little Learned Military Horse, star of the first circus in England, two hundred years ago. Roy had heard of him, of course, as people have heard of Adam and Eve.

He and Hans and Little Learned wandered off, swapping show business anecdotes.

Watching Roy's loose-jointed amble, John said to Carrie, 'The old chap *is* a bit down on the right fore. He would have gone lame on the job.'

'Aren't you glad we got him away?' Carrie asked.

'Yes. But—' John reached for a bunch of leaves in the hedge, to have something to do while he said this. 'You do still think that I'm—'

'The best. Always. For ever.'

While John browsed on the hedge, Carrie lay on his neck like a drowned corpse, arms and legs hanging, her face buried in his aromatic mane.

thirteen

Mr Mismo came back from the Isle of Wight the next day. Carrie and Lester found him and Michael crouched in the pigsties, just the top of the green hat showing over the wall.

'Pygmalia!' They vaulted over the wall, and crouched down with him to look through the bars of the farrowing pen. Twelve white piglets like maggots were squeaking round the brooder lamp Mr Mismo had rigged up, to attract them away from their clumsy mother.

'Andrew, Bartholomew, James, John, Philip, Thomas . . .' Lester started to name them after the twelve apostles.

'Hold on,' Mr Mismo said. 'There'd better be some sows in that lot, if I'm to increase my stock.'

'Phillippa, Thomasina, Joanna . . .'

'I call them the Twelve Dancing Princesses.' Mr Mismo was very romantic about pigs. 'Good thing they didn't dance into the world last night, with no one here.'

'We did check,' Carrie said. 'Quite late. On our way home from – home from . . .' She stopped. Lester poked her and she lost her balance. She picked herself up from the mud of the sty and said, 'On our way home from – I mean, we came to tell you – well, it's like this.'

'Cough it up, old chum,' Mr Mismo said. 'Better out than in.'

'There's a horse in your calf pasture,' Lester said airily.

'There isn't, you know.' Mr Mismo stood up, his knees cracking like pistol shots. 'Till some of my old girls start calving, it's empty.'

'It was.' Carrie tried to stretch a charming smile, but it felt more like a stiff grimace.

'All right, all right.' Mr Mismo had known her long

enough to get the message. 'Come on then, let's go and look at it, and you can think up a good story on the way, Rover.'

Because all Carrie's animals had people's names, Mr Mismo had decided to give her the name of a dog.

'What a whopper,' he said when he saw Roy. 'He's as big as that Clydesdale I won the championship with at the County Show.'

Mr Mismo's past seemed to be full of championship horses of every variety, to suit the occasion. 'Used to pull the old wagon, that horse did. Just like you or me. Took him right out of the shafts and put him in the show ring, and he beat the best of 'em. "For quality, I can't fault him," the judge said—'

'You've got it!' Lester interrupted the flow, which could go on for half an hour, when Mr Mismo's pale blue eyes took on that faraway look. 'Roy is a farm horse.'

When they smuggled Peter away from a rotten home, they had disguised him with black hair dye. They took Roy back to Mr Mismo's farm, and plastered him with gummy mud from the pig wallows.

There was a lot of him to plaster. He looked like a hippopotamus.

Michael ran in from the road where he had been on watch with the lanky hound Gilbert.

'I just saw Arthur.' Arthur was the sneaky boy who worked for the Post Office, the village busybody who knew everything about everybody, and none of it good. 'He said a man in a red car is asking about a lost grey horse.'

'What grey horse?' Carrie picked up some hay from the yard and stuck it in Roy's darkly bedraggled tail.

'So Arthur told him to go and ask the Fieldings. That's us,' Michael told Roy, standing on tiptoe to slap a lump of mud on to the horse's broad chest.

Carrie ran to warn Mr Mismo. He came to the back

68

door, eating a bath bun. He ate all the time, chain-eating, like chain-smoking.

'Discretion is the better part of you know what, Rover. Come down, Rita!' He bellowed up the stairs for his wife. 'I want you to drive me into Town.'

Mr Mismo had lost his driving licence for running into the war memorial, which was a merciful relief for public safety.

'I took you yesterday!' his wife bellowed back.

'This is today!'

When they had gone, Lester and Carrie put the dusty harness on to Roy and hitched him to the old blue cart. He had probably never been in harness, but he was a horse you could do anything with. If he came through this, Carrie was going to teach him to count, like Clever Hans, fake or no fake. She urged him forward. He felt the weight of the cart and hung back, but as soon as he understood, he threw his massive shoulders into the collar, and pulled the cart up the slope to Mr Mismo's turnip field.

He stood by the long, straw-covered mound of turnips, resting a muddy leg, the cracked blinkers on the bridle standing out at right angles from his dirty, patient head.

'He's here!' Michael and Gilbert raced up from the road, and went to ground under a tarpaulin. Lester and Carrie hid behind a straw stack. Rodge, muddied from foot to head, including his beard, and much more like a farm worker than a music teacher, rolled up his sleeves and started to throw turnips in the direction of the cart. Some went in. Some missed.

It was Ma Rosinella's son.

'I'm looking for the Fieldings.'

'They're not here.'

Thump, thump. Two turnips in the cart. 'Oi, look out!' That one must have hit Rosinella.

When he asked, 'But do the Fieldings live here?' Rodge,

good old Rodge, boldly answered, 'Yes,' to keep him away from World's End. Carrie and Lester let out their anxious breath on a sigh of proud relief that he could tell a good lie without stammering.

'I'm looking for a horse,' Rosinella said. *Here it came.* 'About the size of that poor old skin of yours.' *Phew! There it went.* 'You never heard of a curry comb?' he asked rudely. 'That nag looks like the wrath of God.'

'Never having expa-expa-experienced God's wrath,' Rodge stammered placidly, 'I wouldn't know.' Thump, thump, and a thud, squelch, as a turnip hit Roy's imperturbable quarters and bounced off.

'With all this unemployment about,' Rosinella said, 'I'd have thought the Fieldings would give the job to someone who could see what they were at.'

'It's Hire the Handicapped Month,' Rodge said sweetly.

'I beg *yours*,' Rosinella said, and went away.

fourteen

When Lester, who had a network of informers like the C.I.D., heard from one of his spies that the circus was pulling up stakes to move on, they took Roy back to World's End.

He settled in happily with John and Peter and Oliver. Leonora and Sebastian made friends with him over the orchard fence. Oliver, who had no idea how small he was, attached himself like a pilot fish to the big horse, who stood about six hands higher than him. He grazed alongside, turned when Roy turned, an absurd parody of Liberty horses.

Wendy liked the big grey horse too.

'Where's Roy? Come on, let's find Roy in the stable.' Her tail waved like a banner as she led Rodge fast to the loose box Carrie had rigged up with bars across the cart shed, where Roy dreamed his dreams of the sawdust ring, with Dianne and Currier, the oldest hens, roosting venerably on his ample back.

When Rodge could not find Roy in the stable, or Carrie either, he said, 'Where's Carrie? In the field. Come on, good girl, let's find Carrie and Roy in the field.'

Wendy learned to lead him between the trees behind the house, avoiding the hammock, which had once caught him in the chest and felled him. They followed the fence to the flat corner of the field, where Carrie practised bareback riding on Roy.

Lester was better at it than she was, even without practising. His feet, which were smaller than Carrie's, clung like the kinkajou's toes. His light, springy body could balance and turn, and sway easily to the movement of the horse.

But having proved he could do it, he jumped down, patted Roy, and said, 'That's enough.'

'Put me up.' Carrie reached her hands up to Roy's high withers, and bent her left knee for a leg up.

'He's sick of it.' Lester put his hands in his pockets.

'He's not. He loves it.'

'You want him to love it,' Lester said. 'Let him make up his own mind.'

'He feels comfortable going in circles. It's his vocation.'

'It was. But we rescued him from it, remember?'

Lester walked away, following a field mouse through the long grass, so Carrie led Roy to the fence and climbed on from there.

Now that the old grey percheron was getting plenty of rest, he seemed to be quite sound. Carrie could only do about one and a half circles anyway, without falling off, or jumping off before she fell. Then she had to take Roy to the fence to get on again.

Michael had made her a surcingle out of old inner tubes from the Peaslys' garage, with a suitcase handle fixed in the middle. She had a rope attached to it to steady her when she stood up, but she spent more time on her hands and knees, hanging on to the handle or the flopping mane, while the broad back heaved gently under her, like the sea.

'Look at me! Look at me!'

One day, she did three circles standing up, and let go of the rope on the last one.

'Look at me! Oh Rodge, I wish you could see me.'

'I can hear it when you fall off.' Rodge was sitting on the fallen tree, carving hearts on it with a penknife.

'That's most of the time.' Em had taken the silver cat, Joan of Arc, up a tree to watch.

'Give me a chance.' Carrie pulled Roy up by the reins which lay loose on his neck. 'When I get better at it, I'm going to give an exhibition. People will pay to see me.

"The Great Carriella and her Wonder Horse Roy in Breath-taking Feats of Daredevil Daring." '

'I thought the wonder horse was supposed to be retired.' Em grumbled.

'He'll make a come-back. Positively his last appearance on any stage.' Since the World's End money had been spent to rescue Roy, it was fair that he should earn some of it back.

Carrie set him again on the trodden ring of turf. She told him, 'Canter!' and stood up, her bare feet trampling his rump. When she got her balance, she dropped the rope and spread her arms, as Lester had done. For about a minute, it was marvellous. Tongue between her teeth, arms out, fists clenched, she kept the balance, the rhythm, to the rocking canter. She was one with the horse moving under her feet, as she was one with John when she rode him well.

Charlie had enough sense not to waste energy following a horse that was doing circles; but Henry the ram was close behind Roy's feathered heels, his own private circus, thin front legs hitting the ground together, stiff and straight, in the stilted way a sheep canters.

Carrie's long hair flopped like Roy's mane. She felt that she was floating, flying, high above the ground. Henry swerved sideways from a cat in the grass. Roy saw him out of the corner of his eye and side-stepped. Carrie fell off and bit her tongue.

'Who'd pay to see that?' Em asked Joan of Arc.

Perhaps she was right. Em often was, although Carrie would not admit it. But the Vicar was planning a Spring Fayre on his lawn, to herald the opening buds, and he said that Carrie could give a bareback riding show and pass the hat, and split the profits with The Old Folks' Outing Fund.

There was an open piece of grass by the fence that

divided the lawn from the churchyard, where the Great Carriella could perform daredevil feats for the breathtaken spectators.

'Do it with me,' she urged Lester. 'We could be a double act, like Rosinella and his wife.'

'No.'

'Why not?'

'Because.'

'Please, Lester. Roy's sound as a trivet.'

'No.'

Carrie even tried saying, 'You're better at it than me,' but Lester hunched his shoulders and said, 'Leave me alone.'

'You could be the Great Lesterola, with his—'

'Shut up.' He turned, swift and fierce. 'It would be like the circus, don't you see?'

'Oh.' Carrie stepped back with a hand to her mouth. 'I forgot.'

He had been a circus elephant, and they had laughed at him. He would never forget.

She began to take Roy up by herself to practise at the end of the churchyard.

After Rodge and Wendy had been there with Carrie several times, and they were not in the stable or the meadow, the diligent, sensible dog learned to take him through the gap in the stableyard wall, along the path through the fields behind Mr Mismo's farm, over the piece of waste land to the edge of the village, across Church Lane, and through the gate of the churchyard, picking her way carefully among the graves.

At the far end, Rodge's hands felt for the weeping angel who kept watch over the tomb of a child. He would sit down on the moss-grown stone, and do what he called watching Carrie practise.

'Look at me!' She liked to have his company. She could

tell him what she had done right, and he couldn't see what had gone wrong.

He brought his accordion, and fitted a waltz to the beat of Roy's cantering hoofs.

'O Danube so blue, so blue, so blue.
O Carrie on Roy, like glue, like glue . . .'

A Musical Ride. Carrie was going to wear a sort of Robin Hood costume she had found in a trunk in the attic. Moth-eaten tights, and a faded green cloak, and a pointed hat with a feather.

'How much do you think we'll make?' she asked the Vicar.

'The Morris Dancers made four pounds last year,' he said, 'but they had bells on their legs.'

Mr Mismo's nephew had brought him a set of sleigh bells from America. Roy should wear jingling sleigh bells on his broad chest, if that was what the public wanted.

fifteen

All week, people in the village had been saying that the Vicar was mad to have an outdoor fête at this time of year, but the morning of the Spring Fayre looked hopeful.

There was warmth in the sun. The only clouds were small fat white ones, far away on the horizon. The sky was that special first clear blue of spring that makes your heart ache with joy at the promise of summer.

Carrie got up very early to give Roy a bath. No good washing him the night before, because, like all grey horses, he picked the dirtiest places to lie down, indoors or out.

The bath was a matter of many buckets of soapy water, and stepladders, and Liza's shampoo for the mane and tail. Michael stood underneath the vast airship swell of Roy's stomach, and swished the dish mop back and forth, as if he were painting a ceiling.

Carrie was excited and nervous about the Musical Ride. Would she fall off? Would she be able to do the difficult jump and turn, teetering for a moment facing the floating tail, before she jumped round again to the security of the flopping mane on the crested neck?

Would Rodge get there in time? He was giving piano lessons, and couldn't catch the early bus. How much would people throw into the hat? How many people would come to the Fayre anyway?

Because her nerves were strung high, she was giving orders to everyone, including Lester, when he came over to help.

'If you're going to boss,' he threw down the tablespoon he was using for a hoof pick, 'I'm not going to help.'

'Don't then.' Carrie was on Roy's back, combing out his mane.

'He's half my horse.'

'All right, you can wash the back half.'

'Don't do the show, Carrie.' Lester stood in front of Roy's chest, with his arms spread wide to reach round the horse's shoulders.

'Why not?'

'You're scared.'

'Pooh, what of?' She looked down at Lester's bony brown face, black hair against Roy's grey neck, and saw that he was serious. 'Yes. Yes, I am,' she said, suddenly serious too.

'Don't do it.'

'I must.'

Carrie was the only one who had not put anything into the red crock for weeks. No one had said, 'You shouldn't have used all that money you got for the radio to buy a horse.' No one had said, 'We need another horse like we need a hole in the head.' If they had, she could have fought them. As it was, she had to do something to make it up.

Lester knew this. 'Rather you than me,' he said quietly, and bent to pick up Roy's enormous hoof again.

Everyone was going to do something at the Fayre, and the Vicar, who understood about the terrible threat to World's End, was going to let them all keep half of what they made.

As well as accompanying the Musical Ride, Rodge was going to be a strolling musician, serenading ladies with his guitar, and playing 'O Sole Mio' on his accordion in the tea tent.

Liza was selling homemade bread and cakes. She had been baking for days.

Tom was going to run the coconut shy. Michael would pass the hat for Carrie and Roy. Em was going to sell stuffed eggs, her speciality this season, since the hens were laying like lunatics.

Because Liza would not let Em near the stove when she was baking, Michael had hard-boiled the eggs in a cauldron, which was a bucket hanging from the cross bar of the laundry lines over a fire in a ring of stones. He was practising for living rough as a refugee, if Uncle Rudolf ever did turn them out.

'Hubble, dubble, toil and bubble;
Fire burn and clodrun dubble.'

He chanted like the three witches in *Macbeth*, which he had been reading to Miss Cordelia Chattaway.

'Eye of noot and toe of fog,
Wool of bat and tunj of dog . . .
For a charm or powful tubble,
Like a hell-borth doil and dubble.'

His twigs were damp, and the fire gave out more smoke than heat. Liza ran out and whipped Rodge's clean shirts off the line with a foul oath. The eggs took about four hours to cook.

Em shelled them and halved them, and scooped out the yolks and mashed them up with salt and pepper and curry powder and Worcestershire sauce, and put them back into the whites, and arranged them on one of Michael's trays made from a picture frame, with a soppy picture called 'Lover's Vows' still in it.

Michael had ridden down to the village on Oliver to borrow a top hat from a friend of his who did conjuring tricks, to collect the money for the Musical Ride.

He came back at a gallop, wearing the hat down over his ears and eyes.

'Disaster has struck.' He jumped off in the back garden, where they were collecting things to take to the Fayre. When he pushed back the hat, his eyes were round with

78

horror under the straw-coloured fringe which he had cut across with the stable scissors, to match the style of Oliver's forelock.

'Uncle Rudolf and Aunt Val are here,' he said. 'I saw them come out of the Estate Agent's.'

'Oh no. Not today.' Carrie couldn't bear them today.

'And worse.' Michael's voice dropped down to where his boots would be if he had not been barefoot. 'Rose Harbottle is in the black car.'

'Oh *God!*' Em said. Tom would not let her swear, but he and Liza were on the Vicar's lawn, helping to put up the stalls.

Rose Arbuckle was Aunt Valentina's drippy friend, a drag, a moaner, a failed person, who had once announced that she should have been drowned at birth. No one had disagreed.

'Perhaps they won't come here, if—' Carrie started to say, when Aunt Val's ringing 'Yoo-hoo!' sounded outside the front door. Lester took off. He always disappeared when Rudolf and Val came. They did not believe he existed.

Everyone at World's End used the back door into the kitchen. The front door had not been opened for weeks, and was stuck from the rain. They could hear Uncle Rudolf banging on it with the handle of his umbrella, and shouting, 'Open up!' He pounded with his fist, and finally kicked open the door with a splintering crash.

Aunt Val went on a tour of the house, as if it was hers. Which it was, but it was none of her business whether beds were made or clothes hung up, or there was a baby caribou in the warm place by the chimney, or a sick rabbit in a shoe box on the sitting room mantelpiece.

From her cries of, 'Oh, disgusting!' and, 'Savages!' and, 'Living like pigs!', and, 'I am going mad!', they could trace her passage through the house.

She emerged from the back door as if she had come

through a nasty experience, wrinkling up her painted face, and brushing off her clothes.

'The sooner the better,' she said to Uncle Rudolf. *Sooner the better what?* 'It's falling to pieces.'

'Did you break down the door, Uncle Rhubarb?' Michael asked.

'Don't call me that. It's broken already. The whole thing will have to come down anyway, if the developer's plans go through.'

'What developer?' Em asked.

'What plans?' Carrie asked.

But Uncle Rudolf had turned away to poke his umbrella at a bulge in the hammock. The bulge was the black and white half Siamese cat, Paul. He jumped out with a yowl. Em picked him up and stood with her chin on his back, her vivid blue eyes glaring at Uncle Rudolf, as the cat's green eyes glared.

Aunt Valentina's friend, Rose Arbuckle, who was always shedding bits of herself, hairpins, scarves, bracelets – she had lost her upper teeth once in Em's marble cake – had stayed in the car to look for her gloves.

She staggered round the side of the house in her tottery heels. 'I'm such a nuisance. No one should wait for me.' They hadn't. 'Don't bother about *me*. Oh goodness, I'm nobody.'

She fell into the ditch that Tom had dug at the end of the drainpipe, and stood with one leg in the muddy hole, wailing feebly.

'Now you know what it's like to have one leg shorter than the other,' Michael said, as he helped to pull her out.

'I know nothing,' Rose lamented. 'I never shall. I've been a nuisance all my life.'

'You can say that again,' Aunt Valentina told her crossly.

'You won't believe me,' Rose Arbuckle said. No one ever did. 'But in the lane, I saw the most pitiful sight.'

The drop on the end of her long nose quivered with emotion. 'I saw a man walking along, leading a poor blind dog.'

Poor old Rose. She got everything backwards. She would put her shoes on the wrong feet if you didn't watch her.

'Thank goodness you're here.' Carrie ran to meet Wendy and Rodge, wearing his accordion slung round him, and squeezing out a little tootly tune as he came round the house. 'I was terrified you'd miss the bus.'

When she introduced him to Rudolf and Valentina, Aunt Val said, 'Good morning,' in her bad-smell voice for talking to hippies and weirdos, because Rodge wore a beard and a pair of bleached dungarees, patched by Em with daisies and Peace signs. 'Is he blind?' she whispered to Carrie.

'Yes, but that doesn't mean he's deaf.'

'Has he come to tune the piano?' Aunt Val only knew of a few things that blind people could do.

'And he's not half-witted either,' Carrie said, 'so you don't have to talk about him as if he wasn't there.'

'Look, it's a guide dog!' Rose Arbuckle clapped her hands, as if she had made a unique discovery. 'Oh, look at the lovely doggie. I wish I was blind,' she babbled to Rodge, who was blushing and stammering and being shy all over again, 'so I could have one of those lovely doggies.'

Poor old Rose.

sixteen

Uncle Rudolf had come to tell them that he was sending a surveyor to World's End to measure the land.

'But you said you'd wait till Dad gets back,' Carrie protested.

'I said nothing of the kind. If the new by-pass goes through, a lot of people will want to move out this way, and I can't afford to miss the market. Land to build on ... little modern houses, roads ... electricity ... plumbing ...'

Carrie put her hands over her ears.

'... street lights ... petrol stations ... a shopping centre ...'

It was Em who cut short the terrible words. Still clutching Paul, she stamped her feet in front of Uncle Rudolf, her wild curls on end and her eyes blazing.

'You can't!' she shouted. 'You can't sell World's End to anyone but Dad!'

'My dear girl.' He took a step backwards. 'He could never pay my price.'

'He'll bring lots of money back,' Em said. 'And we're all saving. I get jobs. And Tom and Liza work at night. And Michael's got a million pennies from Miss Chattaway. And Carrie's going to give a circus show at the Spring Fayre this afternoon.'

'Oh, I see.' Aunt Val smiled. 'I thought she was dressed like that because she had no other clothes.' Carrie was wearing the Robin Hood costume. 'Are you really going to perform in that ridiculous get-up?'

Carrie had felt all right. Now she wanted to fall into the grass, and be swallowed up by the kindly earth for ever.

'It really is rather pathetic, Rudolf,' Aunt Val said, in

the amused voice which was the nicest one she ever used for the children. 'These poor, absurd kids. I suppose we ought to run into Town and buy the girl a proper circus costume.'

Carrie said, 'No!', which made Val say, 'Yes, I think we should. Come on, Carrie.'

'There's no time.' Carrie held back.

'Yes there is. We'll be back long before afternoon.'

Carrie didn't want to go. But now she didn't want to wear the Robin Hood costume. Aunt Val had laughed at it. She looked down at the droopy cloak, the holey, wrinkled tights.

All right, it *was* ridiculous. She tore off the cloak and hung it on a tree. She threw the pointed hat into the hammock.

'Come on then.' She banged into the house to pull on a jersey and jeans, and went out to the car.

It was like a nightmare. It was like one of those terrible dreams when you have to catch a train, and the more you hurry, the later you get.

You can't find your clothes. You can't pack. You can't find the way to the station. Hurry! Hurry! But you can't run. You can't walk. You can't even lift your feet.

Later and later and more and more desperate – you wake, and sink through the bed with relief that the dream was not true.

But there was no waking from this.

Carrie kept saying, 'I'll be late, I'll be late for the show. Please let's go back. Where's Aunt Val? Oh, *please—*'

After she bought the clown costume for Carrie, Aunt Val remembered all sorts of things she needed. She was in and out of half a dozen shops. 'Stop here a minute, Rudolf. Shan't be a sec. Plenty of time.'

'Oh, please. Oh, please.' Carrie's nails were worn down

to the quick. She flung herself about in the back of the car, chewing the ends of her hair.

When Valentina was done at last, she and Rose Arbuckle were getting into the car. There was just enough time, if Uncle Rudolf drove like the wind, to get home, put on the clown costume, climb on to Roy and charge over to the churchyard. Rose Arbuckle tripped over the kerb, bumped her head on the car, and announced that she was dizzy and must go to a hotel and lie down.

'Take me home first,' Carrie begged. 'I've got to get home.'

'How *can* you, child?' Valentina turned round angrily from the front seat. 'With poor Miss Arbuckle in such a state.' ('Nothing but a drag ... always my fault ...' from Rose's corner of the back seat.)

'But Aunt Val, I'll be too late!'

'You're the most selfish, ungrateful child I ever met.'

With a sob that had no tears, Carrie thought of Roy, of Rodge and the accordion, of Michael with the top hat, of the money. It was still a lovely day. There would be crowds ...

Uncle Rudolf stopped for a red light. Carrie opened the car door and jumped out.

She heard Aunt Valentina's cry of, 'Come back!' as she dodged across the road among the traffic, and ran, ran, through the Saturday shopping crowds, until her legs ached and her lungs were bursting in her chest.

On the road towards home, she had run herself to a standstill. She turned and held up a thumb. A lorry stopped.

'Bit young for hitching.' The driver leaned out.

'It's an emergency, life or death.'

'If you say so.' He opened the door, and Carrie climbed into the cab.

The driver wanted to chatter, but she could not talk. She sat with clenched hands, staring at the road, her chest heaving, her breath rasping, pushing the lorry forward with her will.

The only thing she said was, 'What's the time?' hoarsely, as the driver slowed to put her down at the crossroads.

'Just after two.'

Carrie and Roy were to start their show at two-thirty. It couldn't be done. Too late, too late. But she trotted through the wood – it was as fast as her legs would go – rounded the corner, pushed open the white gate, and stumbled across the yard to the cart shed.

The bars were down. Roy was not there.

Carrie pulled on the baggy clown costume over her clothes, clambered through the gap in the wall, and trotted on, through the field, and down the path that led behind Mr Mismo's farm, over the litter of the waste ground, over the stile, across Church Lane among the parked cars, and through the churchyard gate.

As she ran between the graves, she saw the tops of the tents and the coloured flags on the vicarage lawn, saw a crowd at the fence, and some more people on this side of the open space of grass. Heard the accordion, heard Roy's plodding hoofs, and the chink, jingle of the sleigh bells on his chest. Saw Lester – Lester who had so hated the idea of this – high in the air above the turned-up faces balancing and turning, his arms out like wings, his body in an old shirt and ragged shorts graceful as a flying bird on the back of the lolloping horse.

As Carrie panted up behind the group of people who were watching from the churchyard, Lester did a jumping turn, not very well, and a man by the fence shouted, 'Whoops – missed that one!'

Lester's face was set, his eyes fixed on space. He did not seem to hear. But then the man gave a big imbecile guffaw, and the girl with him let out a high-pitched mocking laugh.

Lester paled, and gasped. In a flash of vision, as if she

shared his memory, Carrie saw him in that other circus life, shambling, bewildered.

They laughed at me, because I couldn't do the tricks ...

His foot slipped. He lost his balance, clutched at air and fell, while women shrieked, and Roy went cantering obediently on.

'Get a doctor!'

The gay accordion music stopped. Carrie heard Rodge ask, 'What's happened?'

She pushed through the crowd that had collected at once, like flies. Lester was sitting on the ground with his face twisted, holding his arm and saying, 'It's all right, it's all *right*.'

'Is it?' Carrie knelt down. The arm was limp and strange.

'No.' He looked at her. 'Sorry I messed up the show.'

'But you did it,' she whispered. 'You did it for me.'

'I was up in the hammock tree, and I heard—' he winced – 'I heard Rudolf say ... about World's End. Street lights, plumbing, petrol stations ... I did it for World's End.'

When Liza had taken Lester off to the doctor in someone's car, Carrie went to the fence to see how much money Michael had collected in the hat.

'Why are you dressed like that?' he asked her.

'Like what?' She looked down. She had forgotten that she was wearing the baggy clown costume, red and white, with ruffles at the wrists and ankles. It looked just as silly as the Robin Hood outfit.

Michael stood on tiptoe to pass the hat over the fence. In it, there was two pounds and fifty-six pence, in various coins, a brazil nut, and a plastic badge that said, 'Say Hullo to a Green Plant Today.'

seventeen

That night, Carrie and John and Roy went up to the Star to talk it over with the Little Learned Military Horse.

Because he was a nice friendly little horse, he didn't say, 'It was silly to try it. It takes years to make a bareback rider.' He was clever enough to understand why people do the things they do.

'Horsey people boast that they understand horses,' he said in his funny little precise voice, like a professor. 'But much of the time when the training goes well, it's because the horses understand the people.'

'Did you understand why I took you into the Junior Jumping at that show?' Carrie asked John.

'Because you wanted to win, wasn't it? And we would have, if—'

'Never mind that.' Carrie put her arms round his head, to hush him. Everybody on the Star didn't have to know that she had chucked him in the mouth at the triple bar, and wrecked the whole thing.

'*Mon Dieu*,' Roy sometimes used the French of his ancestors, 'but some people take a bit of understanding, you know. 'I had a groom once, very careless, he used to leave the hay fork in the stable, with the prongs up. Mr Rosinella – he was alive then – he used to rave at him that I would step on it and hurt myself.

' "What a stupid fuss," the groom used to shove me around when the boss wasn't looking, "over a great ugly brute like you." '

'But one day, he stepped on the fork himself, and you could hear him yell for miles. Laugh!' Roy swung his head up and down, with his deep, throaty chuckle. Little Learned giggled, and flicked his curved ears. John snorted.

As Roy moved off to get a drink at the stream, Learned called after him, 'That right fore looks a bit worse.'

'What do you mean?' Roy tried not to favour it, but Carrie had seen, as he stepped through the wet ground near the bank, that he was rather lame.

'I shouldn't have asked you to perform.' She went after him.

'It's nothing.' He looked back over his shoulder. 'Touch of gout. Just old age, my dear.'

He dropped his grey head to drink. On the earth, a drinking horse is instinctively nervous, ears going back and forth, ready to flee if an enemy tries to catch him off guard. On the Star, there were no enemies.

Carrie put a hand on the softest of all places, the little whirl of hair between the ear and the top of the head.

'You're not old,' she said. 'You're in your prime.'

On the Star, it was always light, because nobody needed to waste time sleeping. As Carrie and John and Roy went slowly down towards the darkling earth, Roy did not try to disguise his slight lameness, and Carrie said, 'Even though you're not old, I won't ask you to work any more.'

'Thank you,' he said. He was the politest horse she had ever known. Most horses will step on your toe if you are not careful. Roy would move his big feet carefully out of your way. 'That would be very nice, if it's all the same to you, Miss Carrie.'

John called her She. That was the name he called when he came to her window at night.

Roy continued to call her Miss Carrie, a little bit formal, very polite.

Next day, the postman stopped his van in the lane, and blared his horn. Since Gilbert had moved in, he would not get out of the van.

'It looks like a wolf,' he complained, when Carrie and

Michael and Gilbert bounded down the millstone path.

'But a wolf,' Carrie informed him, 'has a narrower chest and a turned-in elbow. That's how you can tell it from a dog.'

'You don't say.' The postman handed out a postcard, and rolled up the van window, just as Gilbert rose up, slavering amiably, to put his paws inside.

The card said:

Michael understood the message at once. He could read hieroglyphics better than proper words.

'It says, "Not home for some time."' He took the postcard to Tom. 'Will that be too late for Uncle Rhubarb?'

'I'm going to write to them,' Carrie said. The day had started well, with a fine mist rising from the cobwebbed grass, and the postman's van stopping at World's End, but now she felt depressed.

It was marvellous living on their own, free and independent; but it was marvellous when Mother and Dad were here too.

'I'm going to write and tell them to come home soon.' Carrie gouged moodily at Dad's broad initials on the table, scraping out the crumbs.

'No,' Tom said. 'Our only hope is for them, and all of us, to get as much money as we can. Write them that.'

So Carrie tore a page off the R.S.P.C.A. calendar and wrote on the back of it:

Your postcard was divinely funny.
Glad you're making lots of money.
We're all working at this end,
To fill the crock to save World's End.

She could only write letters in poetry.

eighteen

It was sordid to have to think of money all the time, but that was what Uncle Rudolf thought about, and you had to fight the enemy with his own weapon.

The zoo hospital was less busy as the baby animals grew older, so Tom signed up to work with the travelling zoo, which went to parks and schools all over the country. The work was harder, and the hours longer, but it meant more pay.

Wildflowers were spreading colour in the fields and woods. Michael picked fistfuls of buttercups and bluebells, and sat with them at the side of the road.

He had painted a sign on a piece of board:

'BAUTFUL WIDFOWRS
STOP HEAR & BY A BUNC.'

Nobody stopped. After a few hours, the buttercups were shedding their bright petals, and the bluebells were dropping limply towards death.

'You killed them.' Carrie came out to where Michael sat in the shallow grass ditch at the edge of the lawn.

'They died because nobody bought them,' he said.

'Why should anybody buy, when they can pick them for nothing, you silly child?'

Carrie was cross because she missed Lester, who had to stay at home with his arm in a plaster cast. Michael stuck out his tongue at her, and walked off to bury the sad flowers.

Next morning, he went out very early, before Carrie was up. In the dripping silence of the wood, he picked armfuls of bluebells. They smelled sharp and clean. The long white stalks came out of the ground cool and waxy. Michael wrapped them in newspaper, and took them into Town on the early bus. All morning, he stood in the gutter, holding out bluebell bunches that drooped in a sticky curve. Nobody stopped, except Lester's mother, who put him in her car and brought him home.

Two wasted days of the Easter holiday. Michael went back to Miss Chattaway, and the musty books, and the pennies she gave him to put in the red flour crock.

The last handful of pennies was the straw that broke the camel's back. The string gave way. The crock fell into the guineapig's box on the kitchen table – thud on the straw.

'Treacle!' It was Em's guineapig. At the noise of the crock falling, she rushed into the room with a stricken face.

The crock lay on its side in the straw, with coins and notes spilling out of it. Treacle was somewhere underneath. He must be crushed to death.

Em and Michael exchanged a sick look. Neither of them wanted to lift the crock. Expecting to see something ghastly is even worse than seeing it.

They looked at the crock again, and began to cry.

'What's happened?' Rodge came in from the front room, where he had been playing hymns on the jangly piano that had mushrooms growing on the mildewed felts, and would only play hymn tunes.

'The crock fell on Treacle,' Em sobbed. 'He's dead. I can't pick it up and look.'

'Sh-sh-shall I?' Rodge rubbed his hands nervously, as if he could feel the blood and the delicate crushed bones already. He wasn't any braver than Em or Michael.

When he put out his hands to feel the table, then the box, then the rounded side of the crock, they were trembling.

Were you looking for something? Charlie strolled in with Treacle in his mouth, soaking with spit, but intact. He was supposed to leave the guineapig alone, but he had an uncontrollable passion for carrying small creatures about.

In gratitude for a life spared, Michael sorted out all the pennies into a brown paper bag, and took them down to the Post Office in the village to change them.

He took them in a wheelbarrow, because the bag was too heavy to carry. It was raining. He left Gilbert on guard by the barrow, and went into the Post Office to ask Bessie Munce if she would change two hundred and eighty-seven pennies into pound notes and silver.

The postmistress was very busy. Everyone in the world wanted stamps or postal orders, and Mrs Morgan from the bakery was sending a parcel to her son in Australia. Bessie Munce weighed it three times on different scales, checked the postage twice in different ledgers, and dropped her glasses in the waste paper bin.

Michael had to wait in line. When he reached the counter, Bessie Munce couldn't see him, and said, 'Yes, dear?' over his head to the next person in line.

Michael stood on tiptoe, and put his fingers, black from counting coppers, over the edge of the counter.

'Would you like to change two hundred and eighty-seven pence?'

'No, Michael. I would not like to.' Bessie Munce put on her glasses and looked at him through the grille.

'But will you?'

'Oh dear, I suppose I'll have to.'

Michael went out, and staggered in with the bulging bag. Bessie Munce raised her eyes in a prayer for patience. Michael put the bag on the counter. The wet paper gave way. The bag burst. The pennies spilled out, and rolled merrily all over the Post Office.

Mrs Morgan helped Michael to gather the coins into her shopping bag. Three wet pennies had gone under the radiator for good. Bessie Munce was fuming, so Michael dragged out the shopping bag, and took it home in the wheelbarrow. He stored the coins under his bed, and put a note into the flour crock, re-hung with stronger string:

👁 O U 284 pens

nineteen

Rodge was collecting money too. The organist at the church was taken ill, and the Vicar was paying Rodge to play for the services. He could have used the extra money himself, but he put it all into the World's End fund.

One evening when he went to practise for a wedding, Carrie went to the church with him.

She was still at a loose end without Lester, after the outdoor things of the day were done. She liked to sit quietly in a shadowy pew, and listen to Rodge's hands bring out of the organ splendid, triumphant music, or sweet tunes like a woman's voice.

When Carrie turned round and looked up, she could just see Rodge's head and shoulders in the lighted organ loft. Since he did not have to look at the keys and stops, he played with his head held high, which gave him a rapt, inspired look. The lights over the organ glowed like a halo round his soft fair hair. He was no longer just Rodge, with his shirt buttoned up wrong, who blushed, and could not say 'Liza', and was afraid of strangers.

By the time he had finished practising, and switched off the organ and the lights and locked the church, it was quite dark.

Wendy had lain with him in the organ loft, and before he put on the harness and lead, he let her run loose with Charlie in the churchyard.

Carrie and Rodge heard them barking at something in the far corner. Rodge whistled, but Wendy did not come at once. They still heard her deep double bark, and Charlie's silly shouting yelps, which he hoped would petrify rabbits and squirrels.

They went through the dark churchyard to find them.

Carrie stumbled over graves and flowerpots, but the dark made no difference to Rodge, feeling his way among the tombstones.

They found Charlie and Wendy scrabbling at the entrance to a burrow, where rabbits, if any, were probably far inside, and laughing at them.

Rodge scolded Wendy quite sternly.

'Don't,' Carrie said. 'It was Charlie's fault.'

'Charlie's not a working dog,' Rodge said. 'Wendy is. She can make mistakes by mistake. She's a dog, after all. But she can't make mistakes on purpose, because she's a guide dog.'

When Wendy heard that the scolding was finished, she put up her ears and tail again, and stood alert and eager as Rodge buckled on the harness. He took hold of the handle and lead, and felt around him with the other hand to see where he was. His hand found the weeping stone angel which kept guard over the child's tomb where he used to sit to watch Carrie practise her bareback riding. It was at the edge of the graveyard. The headstone was part of the wall at this corner.

Rodge ran his fingers over the sad curves of the angel's robes and drooping wings, and down over the headstone.

'That's funny,' he said. 'I never noticed that. Come and look.'

'What at?'

It was a moonless, darkly clouded night. Carrie could see nothing except the vague silhouette of the angel, curving over the curved stone.

'The name. *In undying memory of our beloved little daughter,*' Rodge's fingers read the deeply carved words slowly. '*Charlotte Fraser. Born 1796. Died 1808. Aged 12 years.*'

'*Charlotte Fraser.* C.F.' Carrie's fingers went to the chain round her neck. 'The silver locket Lester found in the attic. Perhaps it was the same girl. Look – C.F. 1808. They must have given it to her the year she died. And then she lost it. And she lost her luck.'

'What's in it?'

'It doesn't open.'

Carrie would not take it off, but as Rodge felt the engraving on the silver heart, his sensitive fingers found the hidden catch, and it sprang open.

'What's in it?' Carrie was whispering, because it was mysterious standing here in the dark, with Charlotte Fraser's grave in front of her, and what she was now sure was Charlotte Fraser's locket round her neck.

'Is it a picture?'

'I can't tell,' Rodge said. 'But I think there's a lock of hair.'

When they got home, the blind man and his dog going even faster than Carrie down the dark path and over the broken stableyard wall, they took the locket under the lamp, and Rodge showed Carrie how to open it.

There were no pictures. Just a small coil of light, sandy hair. Charlotte Fraser's hair? If so, it was about the same colour as Carrie's, unchanged through all the years, because hair doesn't die.

Carrie cut out a silhouette of John's head from a photograph Dad had taken, and fitted it into one side of the locket. It was difficult to do without taking it off. But she had vowed she would never take it off, and she had the feeling that if she did, she might lose the luck, as poor Charlotte had lost it.

She would have liked to put Lester in the other side, because he had found the silver heart, and it had brought them luck at the circus. But she had no picture of Lester. Carrie could not remember ever seeing a photograph of him.

twenty

It was Em who had the greatest luck of all in getting money for the World's End fund.

The makers of Chewitt dog biscuits, for whom Charlie had made television commercials last winter, were branching out into tinned dog and cat food.

They would need some new commercials. The producer telephoned Mr Mismo to ask him to tell Em, when he went by the house to bring in his cows, to ring the producer back. This was the only way he knew to get hold of Em, who was Charlie's handler and manager.

Em and Charlie went back to the farm with Mr Mismo and the cows, and Mr Mismo put through the reverse charge call for her, shouting into the telephone, as he always did. The farther away the call, the louder he shouted. Once after his nephew had rung him from America, he had been hoarse for days.

'Esmeralda?' The producer sounded really glad to hear her. Em lifted herself on tiptoe to the wall telephone, and her heart lifted too. She had missed the excitement of the studio, and the filming, and Charlie being recognized in the street as 'Catchem Charlie,' and the television people smiling at her deep blue eyes and saying she would be more famous than Charlie some day.

'Will that crazy Charlie dog of yours eat tinned dog food out of a bowl?'

Not if anyone was watching him, Em knew. Catching dog biscuits was fun to him, but he would never drop his head and eat if anyone was looking. He could hardly make a television commercial alone in a dark passage, which was how he liked to eat his dinner at home.

But Em was a good businesswoman, and so she said, 'Of

course he will,' and hoped that it would be, as Mrs Reeper used to say about the school plays, 'all right on the day.'

It wasn't all right. Em went with Charlie to London, first class on the train, with Mr Peasly's taxi at one end and a London taxi the other – all expenses paid, including lunch.

In the film studio, they put down a red and white bowl that said 'CHEWITT' on the side nearest the camera, and was filled with dog food that looked good enough to eat. In fact, Em and the others at World's End had eaten much worse looking stuff when times were thin.

It even smelled good. But Charlie dropped his ears and rolled his eyes, and backed away, looking everywhere but at the red and white bowl. He did not even lick his lips.

'He doesn't like it,' groaned one of the Chewitt people. 'I may as well shoot myself.'

'I could hand feed him.' Em squatted down. 'Come on, Charlie, it's good.' She held out a handful of dog food, but he turned his shaggy head away in deep embarrassment.

'Dogs don't have to be hand fed with Chewitt dog food,' the director said. 'They're supposed to go at it like ravening tigers.'

'We could put in some liver sausage.' Em looked up from where she knelt by the bowl. 'He'd go ravening for that.'

'My dear Esmeralda.' The director put a shocked finger to his lips, and glanced quickly round the studio. 'Television commercials are *honest* these days, haven't you heard?'

'You mean that woman's husband *really* bought her a washing machine after she sweetened her breath with chewing gum?' Em sometimes watched the big colour television set that dominated the Mismos' sitting room.

'But of course.' The director did not seem to think it strange. 'And when viewers see Charlie wolfing that mess in the bowl, they're going to know it's Chewitt dog food.'

Em was cleverer than him, although he was a film director, and she was only an author of unpublished books and unproduced plays. Knowing Charlie, she had brought a chunk of liver sausage in her pocket. When no one was looking, she poked it into the middle of the bowl of dog food.

Charlie sniffed, and his ears went up a bit.

'He'll do it now.' Em got up and stood back.

They started the camera. Charlie advanced rather slowly across the floor, which was made up to look like kitchen tiles, put his nose into the bowl, picked out the liver sausage daintily, and backed away.

'Cut!' The director clutched his hair in anguish and yelled. Charlie dropped the liver sausage apologetically on the fake kitchen floor, and crawled under a table.

Em took him home. London taxi, train, and Mr Peasly's taxi.

'You let me down,' she sorrowed to Charlie, when they were safe in the kitchen at home again. But where was safe these days, with the fatal threat hanging over World's End? 'You let us all down.'

Charlie grinned with his lip lifted, and wagged his tail, and dropped his head to a bucket of garbage, which was far less attractive than Chewitt dog food.

Em felt very low. The glamour had gone out of life.

But not the action. As she was sitting gloomily wondering how to tell the others her story of failure without making it sound like failure, there was a furious squawk and chatter from the garden.

Em ran out. A baby bird had dropped out of the nest. Paul, the black and white half Siamese, had it in his mouth. The mother was flying about in great agitation, swooping down to dive bomb the cat, and squawking her distress.

Em made a lunge at Paul, and caught him just as he went under a bush. She dragged him out. He was growling and lashing his tail. The tiny bird, just covered with downy new feathers, lay as still as death in his needle-sharp jaws.

'Murderer,' Em said, not angrily, because she knew he could not help it. A cat was a cat, and he had done what a cat has to do.

Holding him with her elbows pressed into his sides, she managed to pry open his jaws. The bird fluttered out, unharmed. It flopped about on the grass, with the mother still swooping and squawking. It was not strong enough to take off from the ground, so Em put it on a branch, and it flew away higher into the tree.

Em fished in her pocket, and gave Paul the remains of the liver sausage to compensate.

It compensated so well that the next day, he caught another bird, a full grown robin this time, and brought it in through the open window to Em. She freed it, and sent it flying away through the window, and cut a nice piece of the Sunday beef for Paul.

He was so clever. He was surely the cleverest cat ever to be born since the Russian cat Ivanovitch, who married a fox and was king over all the forest animals.

He was clever enough to keep his eye on the Sunday beef. On Monday, Em sharpened the carving knife on the back step, and cut slices of cold meat for supper. She put the dish on the table while she mashed potatoes with the end of a sawn-off broom handle.

While she was at the draining board, she saw out of the side of her eye Paul jump on to a chair, pat with his front paws on the table edge, and reach his whiskered face out to the dish of cold beef.

'Get off that chair!' Em banged the side of the saucepan with the broom handle.

Paul jumped down, but as soon as Em turned her back

to reach for the salt, he was up on to the chair – a flash of swift white paw, and he had hooked down a piece of meat and was growling over it under the table.

Em said nothing. She turned half round to watch. Having finished the beef, Paul licked his lips, licked his paws, and started an innocent washing routine of his back legs and tail. Em turned back to the draining board, with one eye slid backwards to the table. Jump – flash – the swift paw hooked down another piece of meat.

As Em covered the dish, her heart began to lift again to an idea.

The next day, she pedalled to the village on Old Red, and bought a tin of cat food. She opened it, took out some of the fishy mush, and put the rest in the tin on the table.

Paul sat below, busy on the underside of a paw, licking and chewing between the pads.

Em turned her back. Jump – flash – clonk. Paul hooked the cat food neatly to the floor, stuck in his head and began to eat, following the tin as it rolled round the stone floor.

Em went to Mr Mismo's house and asked him to put through a long distance call to the film producer.

The first slogan that was written for the commercial of Paul hooking down cat food with his paw was, 'The Paws that Refreshes'; but everyone in the studio groaned at the pun, including Em.

They changed it to, 'Chewitt Cat Dinner. Grab it any way you can.'

And there was Paul, in the studio kitchen, with an open tin of cat food on the table. The actress who played his owner turned her back. Paul jumped, flashed out a paw, and the camera moved in for a close up of his face stuck into the tin of Chewitt Cat Dinner on the floor.

Afterwards, there was to be a shot of him thanking his owner. Em had been dying to act that part, but although they were still telling her she would be famous some day, they didn't seem interested in making her famous *now*.

The part was played by a middle-aged actress got up to look like one of those sweet, silly old ladies who are supposed to dote on cats. Paul hated her. He would not stay on her lap for a second, much less reach up to her face for a whiskery kiss.

But months later, when the commercial was shown, there was Paul kissing the actress – actually nuzzling at the side of her face.

'Chewitt Cat Dinner. He'll love you for ever.'

'How on earth did they make Paul do that?' Carrie asked, when they were watching on Mr Mismo's set.

'He's a good actor.' Em held Paul on her lap. He stared unblinking at the lighted screen.

'Oh rot. Cats can't act.'

'I told him what to do,' Em said. 'He'll do anything I tell him.'

'Oh shut up,' Liza said. 'Cats don't do nothing that nobody tells them.'

'It's done with lights and mirrors,' Tom said. 'It's a trick shot.'

'It's not, so nyah.' Em stroked Paul's sleek black back and smiled smugly. 'They put a shrimp in the woman's ear.'

twenty-one

Carrie and Lester spent a week of the holiday with his Aunt Lilian. Lester was still peaky after the accident, and his mother thought a few days by the sea would set him up.

And he did get set up, in business with Carrie at the snack bar on the pier. The owner's daughter had gone abroad, and Lester and Carrie were to wash up, and pick up litter, and chop pickles and scoop out ice cream, if they could get their nails clean enough.

Lester was not supposed to use his broken arm, but as soon as they were on the train, he had taken it out of the sling, and he could do almost everything with it in the plaster cast.

At first, there wasn't much to do. The sea was cold and grey, and the wind stung sand into your face. Aunt Lilian's beds were damp, and her spoons and forks tasted of gravy, whatever you ate with them. The long empty beach was useless without a horse.

But the lucky chance of the job at the snack bar made it all worthwhile. Good pay, and tips. Carrie and Lester were to work every day. This time, they would go home with money for the red crock.

Aunt Lilian's house was outside the town, along the shore. On their first day at the snack bar, Carrie and Lester walked to work on the wide curve of beach, littered with the flotsam of last night's high winds, which had shaken Aunt Lilian's house like a giant with a matchbox.

In a few months' time, this beach would be full of people, browning or blistering, the water dotted with heads, the edge of the sea trimmed with a band of splashers and shriekers. But on this raw and stormy morning, with the mist blowing in from the sea like rain, the shore was deserted and primeval. You could imagine how England must have looked to those first invading Romans two thousand years ago, where there were no houses or people along the desolate coast.

And no bottles or tins either. Lester kicked at bits of rubbish on the edge of the sea. Every high tide brought in its offering of human mess.

But last night's tide had brought in something else.

Something black and tarry lay among the seaweed and beer cans of the tidemark. Lester went ahead to see what it was. He peered, knelt down, and yelled against the wind for Carrie.

It was a big sea bird, choked, smothered, unrecognizable. The head and wings and all the feathers were covered with black oil. The feet were stuck under the tail.

Lester stood up and looked out to sea. There was nothing to be seen on the choppy grey water, but somewhere out there, a deadly oil slick must be trapping the offshore birds.

'Look, there's another!'

At the edge of the sea, a blackened body washed about in the surf. Carrie ran. It was another big bird, still alive. Just alive, exhausted, the feathers on its breast stuck together, exposing the down over the fluttering heart.

Carrie knelt by it, and put her hand out, but did not touch it. The bird's round eye looked at her blankly. She raised her head and looked out to where it had come from, her mist-soaked hair blown across her face. She wanted to scream and sob her rage at the polluted sea.

But Lester pulled off the wide knitted scarf his aunt had forced on him, wrapped up the bird, and ran with it to the lone house of the painter that stood at the edge of the dunes.

The door towards the sea was boarded up for storms,

the windows streaked with salt. But in the cluttered kitchen at the back, the painter was having breakfast with a tin mug and tin plates. When Lester knocked on the window and held up the bird, he came to the door at once.

'My God,' he said, without asking questions. 'So it's true.'

He took the bird close to the fire, and wrapped a piece of blanket round Lester's scarf. 'There was a rumour last night that an oil slick had been spotted somewhere,' he said. 'This is an eider. He comes from far out.'

'There's a dead bird on the beach too,' Lester said.

'And hundreds of others, there will be.' The painter was tall and spare, with a stubble of beard and a darkly weathered face that could be any age. 'We'll have to get a search going. Want to help?'

'Of course.' Lester and Carrie spoke together, then looked at each other. The job. The money. But the money didn't seem important at all when you looked at this bird, this dying victim.

In his sea-rusted Jeep, the painter dropped them by the pier to explain at the snack bar, before he drove on to alert the people who would organise the search and rescue.

Lester hung back. He often would not talk to people he did not really know. Carrie went into the snack bar. She was just opening her mouth to ask the owner if she could manage without them, when the woman said, 'Oh dear, you two kids. I hoped you wouldn't turn up. I do feel bad.'

'Why?'

No work today? Carrie stood poised to run out to Lester, and follow the painter.

'Well, I know you want the money, but so does this girl who turned up last night. She worked for me last summer.'

The girl was at the sink at the back, in fringed leather shorts and hat, washing dishes furiously in gallons of hot suds to her elbows. She looked round and grinned triumphantly at Carrie. It was her sink.

'She can have it.'

Carrie and Lester ran back down the echoing pier, and along the sea front after the painter's Jeep.

twenty-two

They worked for two days and a night, with dozens of other volunteers, to find as many birds as possible, and take them to the rescue station, where they could be fed and cleaned, or put to sleep if they were fatally contaminated.

'I thought you were so dead set on earning money to take home,' Aunt Lilian said, when they dropped off a rescue lorry at her house to tell her what was happening, and cram down some gravy-tasting food.

'We were.' Carrie had sent home a postcard announcing the fortune they would bring back. But that didn't matter. Nothing mattered except wolfing some food to keep them going, and getting out again to the birds.

They searched the beach all night. They had torches, and the headlights of Jeeps and Land Rovers, which took the birds to the cleaning station, wrapped in sacks to stop them preening their tarry feathers and swallowing oil.

The wind had dropped, and the sky was clearing. After midnight, the merciful moon came out to whiten the beaches, and show up the black lumps that floated or struggled in from the treacherous sea. There was a desperate, grim urgency in all the searchers, men and women and the children like Carrie and Lester, that kept them going through the long chilly night.

Some of the time, Carrie felt that she was walking in her sleep alone, unaware of Lester or any of the other figures who plodded down the long shore, her boots endlessly dragging through the wet sand, the roar and hush-sh-sh of the sea for ever in her ears.

Then what had been a black rock moved, flopped and floundered, and automatically she darted between the bird and the sea, so as not to drive him back into the water.

The bird staggered up the beach awkwardly, as if he was an offshore bird like an eider or a sawbill, and there was Lester, with a sack and rescuing arms, and a set white face drained of everything but exhaustion.

There was no emotion any more. At first there had been sorrow and anger at each bird dead, or hideously contaminated. Now there was just the job to be done.

At dawn, they dragged themselves home for a few hours of sleep. Aunt Lilian, who had a son in the lifeboat service, and understood battles against the sea, woke them as she had promised.

'Though Lester's mother won't like it,' she told Carrie, whose tired eyes fought to cope with the sunlit breakfast table. 'He's supposed to be here for his own health, not the birds'.'

'Same thing.' Lester stumbled down the stairs, in the rumpled clothes in which he had slept, his hair in dark spikes, his arm hanging heavy in the dirty plaster cast, frayed at the edges like a beggar's rags.

'You're not using that arm?' His aunt put down plates of greasy sausages, fried bread, flabby bacon, and eggs with burned edges and broken yolks. She was a good aunt, but not because of her cooking.

'Of course not.' Lester changed the fork to his good hand, and put the other in his shirt front like Napoleon.

'Your mother will kill me.'

'Then you won't tell her, will you, Aunt Lilian?' Lester said sweetly.

On the second day, they went to the rescue station to help feed the shocked and starving birds with sprats and herring, and to clean off the oil from the ones that might survive.

Outside the building, the corpses of birds were piled up in long rows. Hundreds and hundreds of them. Some had been brought in dead. Others were so badly oiled that an injection of death was the kindest rescue.

Carrie had seen dead animals and birds, but never wholesale death like this. She stood outside the building with her hair hanging over her numb face, and mourned for the lost sea birds.

In the whole of her life, she would never see anything as terrible as this. She felt as if she had lived her life. She felt very old. And yet her hand moved out to take hold of Lester's hand, as if she were very young.

'I want more kids in here to clean birds!' a voice shouted.

'Come on.' Lester pulled at Carrie's hand. 'There's nothing to do here. We're needed inside.'

They worked all day, washing the sea birds with a chemical soap that would remove the tar without too much of the natural oils, rinsing them in a tub and drying them with hair dryers.

Then they tried to stuff bits of fish into their beaks and make them swallow. Some of the birds died of shock before the cleaning was finished. But they would have died anyway if the oil had been left on them. Many of them refused to eat. Even those who were washed and fed, and looked all right in the warm cages, would have to stay a year in captivity before they would recover enough insulating oils in their feathers to live again in their natural home far out at sea.

Carrie held the neck of a big eider duck between the fork of her fingers, while her other hand rubbed in the soap. He crouched still on the bench, not struggling. But when she washed his downy breast, she felt his small heart beating frantically.

When she held him in a towel in her lap while Lester dried him, his heart slowed. His eye was clearer.

'That chap might make it.' The R.S.P.C.A. man stopped and put his hand on the duck's narrow head.

'If he does,' Carrie had an idea, 'could we take him home?'

'They're terribly difficult to care for.'

'Miss Etty would help us,' Lester said. 'She's a bird genius.'

Miss Etty lived near World's End in a house with a tree growing up through the middle, full of the birds she befriended. Anyone who found an injured bird or a fallen fledgeling took it to her. She would know how to care for this duck.

And then they would set him free. Carrie saw herself with Lester on a sunny, breezy beach, with sparkles of light on the points of the waves. She carried the duck. She raised him high, opened her arms, and as he flew out to sea on his great wings, she felt her heart fly with him, rejoicing in life.

'We'll see.' The man's voice brought her back to the reality of the hot, crowded shed, and the duck on her lap, his heavy body warm from the dryer, his eye round and unwinking, showing no thoughts. 'Try and get him to eat.'

Carrie and Lester got some sprats down his long neck, and some chunks of herring. He was going to live. They would take him home, get fish for him somehow – the cats would be furious – get him used to water again, watch him grow stronger . . .

As Carrie held him, his head suddenly dropped on to his breast. He sagged against her. The big soft body was still warm, but in an instant life had left it. Their eider duck was a heavy dead bird in her lap.

Lester carried him outside and laid him with the others. Carrie went back to the bench, and a boy came in with a sack and gave her another bird to start washing.

twenty-three

When Lester's mother had driven her home to World's End from the station, Carrie went straight to the meadow.

Rescuing the sea birds had been a strange and urgent adventure, but behind all the drama and urgency, and the triumph of the birds that were saved, and the tragedy of the birds that died, the horses had run through the steady inward centre of her mind that was never quite without them.

Peter and Oliver and big contented Roy were grazing at the top of the field, but John was down near the gate, as if he knew the time of the train.

Carrie went into the field. He smelled her hands, checking to see if she had had any dealings with other horses, just as Charlie had checked her for strange dogs as soon as she got out of Mrs Figg's car. John blew over her hair, then put his soft, damp muzzle to her face, and they stood and breathed into each other's noses, communicating more things than Carrie could ever express in words.

She went into the house to change into riding clothes, and to start telling the sea bird saga that she would be telling for days, to anyone who would listen.

But as often happens when you have a lot to tell, there was no one at home to tell it to.

There were various notes on the kitchen table, which was the message centre of the house.

'*Out to supper and none of your business who with. Liza.*'
'*That last bit of cake is mine. I spat on it. Tom.*'
'*Gon to do shoping erans in vilge for Miz Chatwy. Luv to anyon who cares. Micale.*'
'*Gone to studio. Back some time or never. Em.*'

112

Studio, what studio? It could not be television dog food commercials again, because Charlie was at home.

Carrie went up to her room, loving the safe and welcoming feel of this old house. The rooms, the passages, the stairs . . . her feet knew every inch of floor, the dips and slopes in the stone tiles, the worn hollow in the door sill, the cracks in the wood. Her hand knew every latch and door knob. It brushed the backs of familiar chairs, and slid up the smooth wood of the bannister that led her up to her own corner room.

The bed greeted her, unmade as she had left it, the exercise book in which she had been writing her *Book of Horses* shoved under the blanket.

It was open to what she had been writing the morning she left:

A week without horses is like a week without food.
How can it do me or Lester any good?
To leave your horse is to leave a part of you.
If I remember John all the time, will he remember me too?

Her riding clothes were on the floor. The horse pictures she cut out of the newspapers and magazines papered the walls. The windows showed her the stable and the sloping meadow. The room smelled of horses and dogs, and of herself.

Uncle Rudolf said that when he sold this land to the developers, he would have the house torn down, and run a bulldozer over where it had been.

Mr Peasly's taxi stopped in the lane with its well-known brake complaint. A door slammed, the taxi drove off, and someone came into the house.

Carrie went down. It was Em. She was wearing decent shoes and a skirt, and carrying Paul in a shopping bag.

'Oh, hullo,' she said casually, as if Carrie had only been away for the day.

('Kiss your sister,' Aunt Val used to say, not knowing that sisters never kiss.)

'Guess what?' Carrie said. 'There was an oil spill out at sea, and there were all these birds, it was awful.' She started in at once to tell her dramatic story; but Em fussed about the kitchen, pouring milk for Paul, picking up dirty plates, shaking dog hairs off cushions like a grown-up, and only half listened.

'Lester and I cleaned about twenty birds. You had to hold their necks in the fork of your fingers like this, and rub soap into them. Then they took them off to stay at the wildfowl sanctuary for a year, until they get the natural oils back in their feathers. We were going to bring one home, but it – we couldn't bring it back, because—'

'Did you bring back the money?' Em was not properly listening.

'What money?'

'The job. Your postcard said, "Getting lots of money".'

'Oh, the job.' Carrie had not thought any more about the snack bar. 'Well, of course, we gave that up to help with the birds.'

Em understood that. Anyone in this family would. But she did not say so.

She said in an airy, sophisticated way, 'Paul and I made twenty-five pounds, as a matter of fact.'

Now that she had been taken up again by the film people, Em got a bit superior, putting on special voices and faces, wrinkling her nose at things – ants in the cornflakes, Michael belching at the table, Gilbert bringing up frothy chewed grass on the doormat – which were a normal part of life.

She wrote the first act of a new play, and put on a skirt

114

of Mother's which reached her ankles, and acted it out to three cats on the woodpile, and Rosie and Rubella roosting on the henhouse roof.

Crossing a bridge after school, she saw some boys throw a kitten into the river. Em slid down a steep bank to rescue it, and had to be fished out herself up the slippery bank, soaked and gasping, her hair in dripping ringlets and her long eyelashes stuck together.

Someone took a picture of her and the wet kitten, and it was on the front page of the local paper. Em was going to be awarded a medal for bravery.

'She can't just save a kitten like anyone else,' Carrie grumbled. 'She has to go and get a crummy medal for it.'

She could not say that to anyone, so she said it to Lester. What did people do who did not have a friend to whom they could say unsayable things?

Em continued to be a bit uppish. When Tom announced that his travelling zoo would be visiting their school in Newtown, she said that it was only for the babies, and would thrill her no more than a glass of tepid pond water.

But when the zoo was set up on the playing field, with farm animals and ponies, and monkeys and exotic birds, Em spent the whole morning at the pony rides. With a rapt and innocent face, she lined up with a crowd of younger children for her turn on the little Welsh pony, was led slowly round in a small circle by Tom, jumped off and ran back to the end of the line to wait for another ride.

She could ride any of the horses at home, any time she wanted to. But she hardly ever wanted to, because Carrie made her ride properly, and told her what she was doing wrong.

What she wanted, it seemed, was to be led round in a small circle on a small pony, as if she were younger than she was.

It was very strange, and rather pathetic. She was no

longer Esmeralda, who made business deals with film producers and travelled alone to London to bring back real money. She was just a little girl enjoying feeble pony rides with a rapt and innocent face.

Carrie had disliked uppish Em these last days; even suffered the sharp pain of a hatred that only sisters can feel. But this morning at school, watching childish Em on the pony, she suddenly felt that she loved her.

When sisters fought, and hated each other, grown-ups invented prophesies like, *'When you're older, you'll be the best of friends.'* Was it possible they might be right?

twenty-four

Rodge went to London for the annual meeting of Guide Dog owners, and took Carrie with him. Or she took him. Or Wendy took them both, whichever way you wanted to look at it.

Since they could not afford a hotel, they were to spend the night in Uncle Rudolf's big ornate house, with the silver gutters and drainpipes that honoured Rudolf's title of 'The Prince of Plumbers'.

When you travel with a Guide Dog, everybody speaks to you. People in crowds mostly walk alone, not even eyes meeting eyes. But today they kept stopping to talk to Wendy, or about Wendy, or to point Wendy out to each other. Carrie had never talked to so many strangers before.

In the carriage, she made friends with a young couple, smartly dressed, with loud, proud voices, the sort who usually made Carrie tip her head forward to hide blushes under her hair, and wish that she could do the same with her hands and feet, which swelled like heated balloons. But because she was with the team of Rodge and his dog, she was prouder than the smart couple, and could answer their questions.

Rodge always stammered with strangers, even when he talked about Wendy, so Carrie gave a lecture on Guide Dog training, which lasted until they had run between the backs of the London houses, and the filthy brick walls closed in on them to squeeze the train into the station.

'You ought to be a dog trainer some day,' the young husband told Carrie.

'I'm going to be. Horses too.'

Carrie and Lester had sworn in blood that they would never grow up, so the question of a career might never arise. But you had to have something to say when grown-ups asked you what you were going to be when you grew up.

There were dozens of blind people at the meeting, and dozens of dogs, all lying quietly by their owners. The only place on earth where you could find so many dogs in one hall together without pandemonium. Wendy behaved beautifully all day, but when Aunt Val saw her standing politely on her front step, ears cocked and tail waving amiably, she went into one of her flurries, and obviously regretted having said that Carrie and Rodge could stay the night.

'Where will that animal sleep?'

'W-w-w-with me.' Rodge followed Wendy into the house, and stood with his head up, looking about him to sense the atmosphere of the wide shining hall, with its stained glass windows and barley sugar pillars.

'I don't want him on my new carpet.' Val never got the sex of animals right, even when she knew their names. She had been calling Charlie 'She' for ages. It was her subtle form of insult. 'Oh dear, I shall have to put you in another room. Oh goodness, now let me see . . . Carrie, you can go in your old room, but don't touch the ornaments or put grubby clothes on the clean spread. Mr Weston—' she never got people's names right either – 'let's see – no, he can't go in the green room because the window's stuck and I'll never air out the smell of dog . . .' etc., etc.

One thing Carrie was not going to be if she ever grew up was a fussing housewife.

While Aunt Val fussed over the dinner, Rodge and Carrie sat uneasily in the easy chairs, with Wendy – 'On that yellow rug, Mr Weston, where his hairs won't show.'

'She's not sh- not sh- not sh-' But Val's hard heels had rattled back to the kitchen before Rodge could get out, 'Not shedding hairs.'

The telephone rang.

'Answer the phone!' Val yelled from the kitchen.

'You answer it,' Carrie told Rodge.

'I'll never get to it.' Rodge had already found out that the drawing room was cluttered with knick-knacks and occasional tables and lamps and stools. He had tripped over a wire, and cracked his shin on the corner of a coffee table. When Val went out of the room, he had rolled up his trouser leg to feel if it had drawn blood. It had.

The telephone went on ringing. Carrie looked at it. Uncle Rudolf was not yet home from the plumbing factory. She didn't want to take a message for him, all wrong, as she used to when they lived here before they found World's End.

. . . and ringing.

'Answer that phone!' Val yelled again.

Carrie crossed the polished floor, rounded the sofa, skirted a whatnot, stepped over a stool to the table where the telephone stood behind a vase of artificial flowers. Just as she put out her hand to pick it up, the ringing stopped. Just as she had finished the obstacle course back to her chair at the other side of the room, the ringing started again.

She went back. 'Hullo?' Aunt Val had tried to teach her to say, 'Mrs Fielding's residence,' but it hadn't taken.

'Hullo?'

There was no one there. She put down the telephone. It rang again. She picked it up.

'Hullo?'

Nothing.

'Is anybody there?'

Yes. Somebody. Somebody breathing. Carrie could hear it faintly.

She smothered it by putting down the receiver, but waited by the table, looking at the white telephone, which sat there so innocently, but held mystery.

'Who is it?' Rodge asked.

'Nobody.'

The telephone rang again. Carrie put out a hand, then hesitated, with her hand in the air. If she counted six rings, there would be a voice.

. . . three, four, five, six – 'Hullo?'

Nothing. She held her breath to hear the breathing. Very slow and quiet, sensed rather than heard, as if the telephone itself was breathing.

She put it down. When it rang again, she did not pick it up.

'I said, answer the phone.' Val came in, wearing a comic frilled apron that said, 'CHIEF COOK AND BOTTLEWASHER'.

'There's no one there. Just breathing.'

'Oh, that's ridiculous.' Val snatched up the receiver. 'Helleaow?' Her social, telephone voice. 'Helleaow, who's there? Are you there?' She shook the telephone impatiently, and took off the social voice. 'I can hear you, you know, so you'd better not play any stupid tricks. I know your sort, and I'm not having it.' Her strawberry lips curled in anger. Her stiffly sprayed hair bristled.

She slammed down the telephone. It rang again before she reached the door, and she turned and snatched it up furiously. 'Now listen, you'd better stop this, because the operator is plugged into my line, and she'll trace the call.'

'Is the operator really plugged in?' Carrie asked.

'No, but they don't know that.' Val's voice was a little shaky, as she put down the telephone and went back to the kitchen.

When the telephone rang again, Carrie took off the receiver and laid it by the vase of garish flowers.

'Why is the phone off the hook?' Uncle Rudolf came home from the factory and put it back on.

'Someone is ringing and not saying anything,' Carrie said.

'Those fools. Not again.'

'Why again? What fools?'

'I don't know – that's just it. I don't know.' Uncle Rudolf sat down, and rubbed his long nose with a long finger, his high forehead creased with worry. 'Someone keeps making these silent calls, and I don't know why.'

'Burglars?' Carrie suggested. 'To see who's at home?'

'Perhaps. Or perhaps just to make trouble. I don't know. London is full of lunatics these days. Oh well.' Rudolf slapped his bony knees and stood up. 'Let's forget it. They can't scare me.'

He poured himself a large whisky and sat down with the evening paper. But when the ringing started again, Carrie saw that his hands gripped the newspaper tightly, and his eyes were not reading. He did not answer the telephone.

The dinner was marvellous. Tomato cream soup, roast chicken with brown crackly skin, mashed potatoes with a well full of butter, tiny green peas, fruit salad with strawberry ice. Wine for Rodge, cider for Carrie. They had not had a meal like this for ages, if ever. It was one of the reasons they had asked if they could stay here.

Rodge left the dining room dizzy with food and drink. Wendy ran him into a twisted marble pillar in the hall, and he skidded and sat down on the polished floor.

'I thought he was a Guide Dog,' Aunt Val said.

'She is,' Rodge said. 'But she's a dog too. She's not a machine. Nor am I. So we sometimes make mistakes.'

'Not much use in *that* then.' Aunt Valentina triumphantly brushed off the whole Association of Guide Dogs for the Blind.

Wendy stood alert, then moved forward.

'Don't come at me, you tricky creature.' Aunt Val jumped back.

'She hears something.' Sitting on the floor, Rodge cocked his head like Wendy, to listen.

Carrie's spine crept. The heavy curtains were drawn, shutting out the traffic and the unknown London night. Was someone outside? There had been no more telephone calls. Was the breather outside in the garden, breathing against the windows, waiting to get in?

In bed in her old room before the others, Carrie at first left the curtains open, so as not to be taken by surprise. Then she got up and drew them closed. Which was worse, if someone was outside – to know or not to know?

She was afraid, but she could not go downstairs. She had tried that once with a nightmare when Aunt Val was having a dinner party, and got blasted back upstairs for appearing among the guests with dirty toenails and shrunk pyjamas.

Carrie could not stay up here alone, so she sat at the top of the stairs. Aunt Val asked Rodge to play the piano, then began to talk quite loudly to Uncle Rudolf while he was playing. Rodge stopped.

'Go on,' commanded Val.

'Wendy hears something.'

'Oh rubbish, that useless dog. Go on playing, Mr Weston. I'm very musical, you know.'

Rodge didn't have the guts to say, 'Then why don't you listen?' He started to play again, a jolly tune Carrie knew he didn't like, but which Aunt Val had ordered. Soon the music put her to sleep. Rodge fell over her when he came up the stairs with Wendy.

In the middle of the night, everyone was woken by barking in the hall. They came down, Val in a flouncy nightgown, Rudolf in striped pyjamas which hung like a tent on his spare frame, Carrie in Mrs Mismo's son's pyjamas, because there had been nothing else at World's End fit to bring to London.

'What on earth is going on, Mr Weston?'

Rodge was by the door with Wendy.

'I let her bark. She heard s-s-someone outside. So did I.'

'Nonsense, how could there be? I heard nothing.' But Val was nervous. Nervous enough, Carrie saw with some surprise, to have forgotten to put in her teeth.

'We did hear s-s-s—'

He was never going to manage 'someone', so Carrie filled in. 'Blind people are better at hearing, because—'

'There. In the garden. Speak, Wendy.'

Her double bark, deep and baying.

'Shut up!' Val put her hands over her ears. 'I can't stand that noise. Go out and have a look, Rudolf.'

'Have you gone out of your mind, woman?' he asked, and she clutched her hair net and said, 'I've had enough to drive me there, heaven knows.'

Rodge opened the door and unclipped Wendy's lead, and she ran out through the shrubbery and across the lawn, with her labrador's deep, baying bark, chasing, hunting. If there was anyone out there, he would think the hounds of hell were after him.

Wendy stopped barking. She came back and rustled round a bit among the bushes. When Rodge whistled, she came back to him, looking mild again.

'I told you.' Aunt Val shut the door, and shot the bolts. 'There's no one there.'

But in the morning when Carrie took Wendy out to run, she found the footprints of a man in the flowerbed underneath the side window.

twenty-five

When she went into the house, there were some letters on the door mat. Carrie picked them up and put them on the hall table. The top envelope had a foreign airmail stamp. A Greek stamp. It was addressed in familiar writing. Her father's writing.

She turned it over, handling the paper that he had handled, seeing him sitting on deck in the sun, dashing off a letter to his brother in his careless scrawl.

The flap was not properly stuck down. Carrie's first two fingers slid under the side of the flap that was unstuck, got into the envelope and held the letter. Not to pull it out, or read it. Just to prove it could have been done, then stick the flap down properly.

She pulled out the folded paper. Not to open it. Just to turn back the top to see the name of the boat – *Mariner*, and the date – two weeks ago. He must have forgotten to post it. The envelope was creased, as if it had been in his pocket, and there was a beer stain in one corner.

Carrie glanced up the stairs. Uncle Rudolf's electric razor was going like a buzz saw. Valentina was singing whoopily in the bath. Rodge would not come down in this strange house until Wendy went up for him.

If she was going to read the letter, she must do it quickly. She read it. She had known all along that she would.

'Dear Rudolf,
Just a few lines from the sun-drenched isles of Greece which today are drenched with nothing but blackness. For me and Alice.

As you know, we've been saving all wages to make a down payment on the house at World's End. Our boss, the

*mad millionaire, has a thing against banks, so pays us in
cash. Wot a luvverly pile. But there are light fingers all
along these shores, so I hid the cash in the pockets of an
old jacket under the bunk. Forgot to tell Alice, and she
gave the jacket to a poor old beggar on the dock. He begs
no longer. Nor is he poor. Nor is he on the dock – or anywhere in sight.*

*I know you're in a hurry to sell. I'm asking you to wait.
Please, Rudy? Don't tell the kids. I'll do that, somehow.'*

Carrie re-folded the letter and put it in the envelope,
licked the gum his tongue had missed, and stuck the flap
down tightly.

She went upstairs like a sleepwalker, her hand on
Wendy's collar, her legs numb, her mind turned off like a
stopped clock.

Her mind was still numb when she left with Rodge to
get the train for home. Aunt Val saw them off quite gaily
from the door – she was always gayer when you left than
when you arrived.

'See you soon!' she called. 'We'll be down next week on
business!'

'Business,' muttered Rodge. 'Is he really planning to
sell your house?'

'It isn't ours,' Carrie said miserably. Thinking of Dad's
terrible letter, tears clouded her eyes, and as she turned
out of the gate, she bumped into a man who had stopped
by the wall to light a cigarette.

She trod on his toe, and he cursed her – 'Watch where
you're going!' and slouched off down the hill.

It was not until she got home to World's End that Carrie's
mind began to work properly again. Rudolf had said nothing about the letter, and she could not ask him. He had
read it at breakfast with an unchanging face, put it in his

pocket, and gone off to the factory without a word.

Would he understand? Would he consider waiting? Would he even answer the letter? What would he make of that unfamiliar *'Please?'* Dad never begged anyone, least of all his brother. *'Please, Rudy?'* He never called him by the nickname of their childhood.

'Don't tell the kids.'

And Carrie couldn't either. They were still so optimistic, collecting money wherever they could for the red crock, still counting on Dad and Mother's rich return before the end of summer, refusing to believe that it might be too late.

How could Carrie tell them, 'It is already too late'?

'I'll do that, somehow.'

Somehow, Dad would find some way to tell his family. Meanwhile, Carrie had this terrible burden. The burden of knowledge, which can be worse than a burden of guilt. Knowledge of disaster, which she could not share with anyone.

Not with Tom, working long hours, travelling long miles, sleeping in the horse box when they visited distant schools. Tom who had said, last time he came home, weary and bleary, to hand over a pay cheque, 'Dad and Mother have never let the family down, and we won't either.'

Not with Liza, who was washing glasses at the pub in Newtown on Saturday nights, to add to her wages from Alec Harvey and the transport café.

Not with Em, who had put all Paul's television money into the red crock, although she was desperate to buy a dress. The school had given them uniforms, but that was all she had, except for Liza's cut down skirt and jeans, and shorts outgrown by Carrie.

Not with Michael, hatching out chickens who might never lay for him, and setting out vegetable plants that he might never harvest.

Not even with Rodge, who was adding to his church

organ money by playing the piano on Saturday nights for Old Tyme Syngynge (his worst musical hate) in the pub where Liza washed glasses.

Rodge, like Liza and all the animals, had found a home here. Carrie could not tell him. He was too happy here. Everyone was happy here. Everyone except Carrie, with her lonely burden of dreadful knowledge.

She told it to Lester. She told him everything. It was like telling it to herself.

twenty-six

How could they lose all this?

With bitter irony, this spring, which might be the last spring, was the best ever at World's End.

The lower curve of the hill pasture was golden with buttercups. Higher up, white flowers starred the turf where the horses grazed in their thinner, shinier summery coats. There was blossom everywhere. Great waves of it hit your nose as you rounded the corner of the hawthorn hedge. The apple trees foamed. Under the cherry tree, you stood on thickly fallen petals and looked through a cloud of soapy pink fragrance into a sky that was blue day after day.

Grass, flowers, weeds, green sprouting hedges, baby animals – everything grew so eagerly that you could almost see it happen.

Michael measured one of Rubella's chicks, and sat for several hours to watch it growing, as he watched Liza's bread dough rising in the bowl at the back of the stove.

When all the chicks and ducklings were hatched, and two saucy kids born to the Nubian goat Lucy, Michael wrote a sign and hung it on the horseshoe knocker on the back door:

THEIR ARE NOUGH 199 LEGGS IN THIS ETABLEMENT.

The days were so warm now that Roy let down his creaky joints to lie flat out to the sun in the field by the barn. Mrs Potter saw him from the road, and stopped her car to run into the yard calling out that the poor old horse had kicked the bucket at last.

Michael made another sign and hung it on the gate between the field and the road:

How could they lose all this?

Every time Carrie went riding over this green and friendly countryside, the thought came, *'It could be the last time.'*

Wherever they went, she would have John, even if she had to smuggle him into a back yard in some awful slummy town. But she would not have the curving grass track where she cantered with Lester round the shoulder of the hill. The plunge into the cool wet woods, trotting on fallen leaves. The scramble over the crumbling wall to gallop across the wide stretch where the old airfield had been – clacketty over the broken concrete runways, muffled drums on the grass – as John raced Peter for the far corner.

Over the common, hopping little gorse bushes. John shying, as a rabbit popped out just at the lip of the steep quarry. Carrie's heart in her mouth at the thought of swerving right over the edge where they said the Headless Horseman still took his neck-breaking plunge when the moon was right.

I hate the dreadful hollow behind the little wood...

Carrie and Lester always chanted the poem as they passed this treacherous place.

...the red-ribbed hedges drip with a silent horror of blood, And echo there, whatever is asked her, answers 'Death'.

They slid down a chalk bank at the end of the common, and on to the road, to walk along by the side of the traffic among the mucky things people had chucked out of cars. Children stared at the horses out of the back windows, pale with envy.

Soon they turned away across the ditch and into the

flat wheatfield where the farmer had left a wide strip under the hedge when he ploughed.

They cantered fast, not racing. John's plain mealy nose level with Peter's delicate chestnut head, the back of his long ears and his dark blowing mane the only view Carrie ever wanted to see for ever.

They cantered easily, not talking, not thinking, into the spring wind, and reached the end of the stubble strip almost without knowing it, as the horses slowed. It was like ... Carrie looked at Lester, bareback on Peter, his dark hair tumbled over his shining eyes. It was like ...

Sometimes they knew that they flew downstairs without touching the steps. They had never talked of it. If they talked about it, it would not happen. So they did not talk about this – that the canter had been like flying.

At home, Lester swung off while Peter was still walking, and he went on into his stable, long chestnut tail swinging like a bell. Carrie dropped her reins, and John stopped.

Beyond the wall, Tom, with a rare day off, was hammering an extra bedroom on to the goat shed, so that the ram could have some peace away from the knobby, butting foreheads of Lucy's kids.

Em and Liza were at the laundry line between the trees, hanging out tatter-washed curtains, and banging dusty mats with old tennis rackets buckled into the shapes of spoons.

The healing sun had warmed away Roy's lameness. In the yard, Michael had leaned the apple ladder against his wide ribs, to scale the heights of his back. When he was on, with his short legs sticking forward over the horse's shoulders because they couldn't get round his sides, he took Roy by the highest part of the wall, where Rodge was sitting. Rodge put out a foot to feel where the horse was, slid a leg over behind Michael, hung on to his waist and they ambled away, swaying to Roy's rolling plod.

The old horse opened the gate with a push of his nose and a shove of his broad grey chest. As they turned down the lane towards the village, with Wendy following close like a dog born to horses, they began to sing 'King of the Road':

'Trai-ler for sale or rent,
Rooms – to let, fifty cents ...'

Michael shrill, Rodge's voice sweet and true.

'I'm a man of means, by no means –
King of the road.'

John turned his head and nudged Carrie's toe to ask if she was going to get off, or sit there all day.

How could they lose all this?

twenty-seven

Carrie did not have to keep her lonely secret for long. Not long enough.

When Rudolf came down to see the developer who wanted the land, he told the others what Dad had written.

He told Carrie too, and she had to look shocked, as if she did not know what was in her father's letter.

Rudolf told it very brutally, in the middle of Michael telling him how much money they had collected: 'And with what Dad brings home, Uncle Rhubarb—'

'Don't call me that. And your Dad will bring home nothing. Nothing do you hear that, boy?'

He told them about the letter. Carrie wished that she had done it herself days ago, so that she would not have to see their faces now, with Rudolf and Val looking on.

No one spoke. After a while, Michael asked from the floor, where he sat with his arm round Gilbert's shoulders, the hound's head higher than his, 'If we can't stay here, where would we go, Uncle Rhubarb?'

'You managed before, didn't you? You'll manage again. Live on a boat with that feckless father of yours. Camp out. Put up tents. Just your style of living.'

'But the animals.' Michael spoke for them all.

'Look.' Uncle Rudolf checked his watch. He had an appointment. 'I didn't ask you to have all these animals here. In fact, I asked you not to, if you remember.'

He put on his hat and went out. He never went out without his hat, even in the car.

They hated him.

Carrie ran outside so that she should not see the others, and so that they should not see her crying. She ran up the hill. It was raining.

'When I crept over the hill, broken with tears,
When I crouched down on the grass, dumb in despair . . .'

John was up there under the lone elm tree. She fell
against him and cried into his wet mane. She wanted to
stay up here for ever, not have to talk to anyone, ever
again. *'Dumb in despair'*, like the girl in the poem. But
she had to go back to the others.

'As I went down the hill, I cried and I cried,
The soft little hands of the rain stroking my cheek,
The kind little feet of the rain ran by my side.'

And Lester. He came through the hedge from the wood,
and ran by her side, as he always did when she needed
him.

When the land was sold and World's End pulled down,
Uncle Rudolf was thinking of retiring from business and
building a posh modern house with an all-electric kitchen
and burglar alarms, to protect him from whoever it was
who threatened him in London.

He went to talk to a builder, while Valentina stayed at
the house to do what she called her 'grand tour of inspec-
tion', as if she were the Queen Mother visiting a hospital.

Liza had the day off, but she went to work at the zoo
with Tom, to get out of the house. The others sat about
without spirit, while Val racketted through the bedrooms,
slamming cupboard doors and fighting squeaky drawers,
opening windows to shake out mats, throwing clothes off
beds into a huge pile, which she pitched down the stairs
with a shout of, 'Someone start washing all this!'

Nobody moved. The clothes carpeted the stone flags
of the front hall.

'Who's been sleeping in your mother's room?' Val
came to the top of the stairs.

'Goldilocks!' Lester shouted back.

'Rodge sleeps there.' Carrie went through to the hall. At the top of the stairs, with her piled up hair and high boots, Val looked seven feet tall, towering over her like the Fates.

'Does *he* live here too, as well as that bad, brazen girl?' Valentina had never liked Liza. Although she sold flags for a prisoners' aid society, she did not like anyone who had actually been in trouble with the police. She didn't like Rodge either, because he had beaten her at Twenty Questions, and Wendy had been sick on her oriental prayer rug.

'He often stays the night here.' Carrie stood in the sea of dirty clothes.

'Doesn't he have anywhere to live?' Val grumbled. 'I knew this place was an asylum for broken-down animals, but I didn't know it was a home for the handicapped as well.'

'Don't Aunt Val—'

Rodge had come through the kitchen, and Carrie waded through the clothes to him.

'I'm sticking out my tongue at her,' she said. So Rodge stuck out his through his beard in the direction of Val's voice, which was back in Mother's room, still carrying on about mud and dog hairs and poor Alice would have a fit. Although Mother always slept with at least two dogs and a cat in her room. One night when John had colic, she had slept in the stable with Carrie, snuggled together in the straw with cocoa and ginger biscuits.

When Carrie was back in the kitchen, there was a knock on the front door. Who on earth—?

'I'll go.' Val put on a high flutey voice, hoping for a social visitor – a vain hope at World's End, thank goodness – and tripped down the stairs. She opened the door, which had unstuck itself in the spring warmth, and they heard from the kitchen a man's deep, rather husky voice. Someone they knew? The voice was vaguely familiar.

'Mrs Fielding?'

'Mrs Rudolf, or Mrs Jerome?' It was amazing how Val could switch from yelling at the family to cooing at strangers.

'Mrs Rudolf.'

'This is she,' Val fluted.

'I've come to tell you ...' The man dropped his voice then, but in a moment, Val came flying into the kitchen, with her face all slipped, and her stiff beehive of hair toppling, as if the man had pushed it.

'It's Rudolf!' she cried, and her voice broke on a hysterical sob. 'He's had an accident with the car. They think he had a heart attack, and he—'

'Is he hurt?' Carrie and Lester and Em and Michael and Rodge had all jumped up.

'A broken leg, at least. He ran into a wall, and they've taken him to the hospital. A plainclothes policeman has come for me in a car. I'm to go at – go at—' Suddenly unstrung, Val dropped in a chair, with her boots stuck out and her face crumpled. 'Go at once.'

'I'll go with you.' Michael put his hand on her knee.

'No, me' Carrie and Em said together. All at once, they liked Val better than they ever had in their lives, and felt pity for her, now that she was softened by tragedy.

But she jumped up and snapped, 'They don't let children into hospitals.' And when Rodge offered, 'Wendy and I will come with you,' she said quite rudely, 'They don't let dogs in either,' snatched her coat off the hook under the stairs, and went out to the policeman.

Same old Val after all.

After she had gone, they did not know how to feel about Uncle Rudolf. Sorry for him, of course, but they still hated him for what he had said to them, and what he was going to do to them.

Did you have to start liking people you hated just because they were smashed up? When he was mended, he would still be the same hateful Rudolf, and it would have been a waste of effort trying to like him.

'Perhaps he will die—'

Michael did not exactly say it. He suggested it casually to Gilbert, but the others jumped on him for saying what they thought themselves.

Rodge was as nervous and upset as they were. He could not sit still. He walked about restlessly in his thick rubber soles, while Wendy turned her head from side to side to watch him, like a spectator at a tennis match. Then he felt his Braille watch and said, 'Oh Lord, the church. I promised I'd go and try out Sunday's music. I'll be back as soon as I can.' He called Wendy to him, and put on her harness and lead, fumbling with the buckle.

'Don't worry,' he told them with a very worried face, and went out, stumbling on the back step, which he had been up and down millions of times.

Lester was supposed to go home, but he wouldn't leave World's End. Even he did not know what to do, what to think, how to feel. None of them knew. They stayed near the house in case Aunt Val came back with news.

When a car stopped in the lane, they all ran out. It was the black car like a funeral hearse. In it was Uncle Rudolf, still wearing his hat dead centre, and with all four limbs intact.

'You had an accident!'

'You had a heart attack!'

'You ran into a wall!'

'You're in the hospital with a broken leg!'

They swarmed into the car all over him.

'Pardon me.' He pushed them away and got out. 'I never felt better in my life.'

'But the accident—'

'What accident? I've not had an accident since I fell off my bicycle at school. My insurance man says I have the cleanest record—'

'They said you had a heart attack and ran into a wall,' Carrie said. 'A policeman came and took Aunt Val with him to see you in the hospital.'

'Oh, my God.' Rudolf staggered backwards and leaned against the car, his face grey and sagging, as if the life were draining out of it. 'So that's what they were after. Those phone calls. They're after money. They've kidnapped her.'

twenty-eight

Kidnapped! Their hatred and fear of Rudolf faded before the drama of the moment. Carrie's stomach dropped like a stone in a well.

'What shall we do?' She stared at the beads of sweat which had broken out on the dome of Rudolf's head.

'I'm going to the police.' He opened the car door, but Lester caught his sleeve and pulled him back.

'You can't.'

'Let me go, boy. My wife is in danger.'

'That's why you can't bring in the police. Kidnappers are desperate men,' Lester said, as if he had known dozens. 'They'll stop at nothing. Even murder. Remember the Billericay hatchet case? If the police hadn't bungled the ambush, that woman would be alive today.'

'I *must* tell them.' Uncle Rudolf tried to pull away and get into the car.

'You *can't*.' Carrie grabbed the other sleeve.

'I must.' But he was yielding.

'You can't.' They took him into the house, and Em put on the kettle.

'What shall I do?' Uncle Rudolf took off his hat. 'Oh God, I don't know what to do.' His face was creased and crooked with anxiety. He looked ten years older.

He put on the hat again, back to front. He paced the floor, chewing his knuckles, pounding his fist into his hand, while the lid chuckled on the boiling kettle, and the others waited, their nerves strung tight, waited for something – they didn't know what.

When the knocker banged, they jumped like electric eels.

The something was Arthur, the boy from the Post Office, leaning on his red racing bicycle and chewing gum.

'Note for Fielding.' He held out an unstamped envelope. Uncle Rudolf snatched it. 'Who gave you that?'

'Well, it's like this.' Arthur blew a bubble of gum, and popped it. 'There's this political meeting going on up the village, see. Joker with a jaw full of marbles telling about how this country is gone down the drain. So I'm there listening, see, and this bloke in the crowd comes up to me and he goes, "Want to make a bit of money?" "Do what?" He goes, "You know the Fieldings?" I go, "Yeah."' Arthur blew a huge disgusting bubble of pink gum that obliterated his face, and popped it with his tongue. ' "Worse luck." "Take this letter," he goes. I go, "Why not post it?" and he goes, "It's urgent, see," and crosses me palm with silver.'

'Well then.' With an effort, Uncle Rudolf kept his voice calm. 'You've been paid. What are you waiting for?'

'For you to open it.' If the letter had not been sealed down tightly, Arthur would have read it as he rode down the lane.

'Right away.' Lester took the envelope, and before Rudolf could stop him, he tore it open with a nonchalant thumb. He turned his back to scan the letter, then turned round with a big grin and said, 'Well, *that's* good news, everybody. Your cousin Maud had twins.'

'Big deal.' Arthur's face fell. He pushed his bicycle round the side of the house and rode off over the lawn, mutilating a clump of daffodils.

'What on earth—?' Rudolf snatched the letter from behind Lester's back.

'Throw him off the scent. If Arthur knew he'd carried a ransom note, you might as well climb the church steeple with a megaphone and tell the whole neighbourhood.'

Uncle Rudolf read the note. He raised his head with a stricken look of horror. The paper dropped from his shaking fingers.

Carrie picked it up. Lester had been right about the police. The ransom note, made from letters cut out of newspaper, said:

Send smallest one with £20,000 cash to phone box behind empty garage on wake road before midnight. If you tell police we kill your wife

'Smallest one.' Michael gave a shudder of excitement, and squared his shoulders. 'That's me.'

'We can't let Mike go!'

Carrie turned to Rudolf, but her uncle spread his hands with the same blank, stricken look.

'Our only hope is to do as they say. We're helpless.'

'It'll be all right,' Michael said cheerfully. 'I'll take Gilbert.'

The great hound panted wetly, and swept his long wiry tail across a low table, knocking a teacup and a milk jug to the floor.

'Grinning Gilbert, everybody's pal,' Em said. 'Fat use he'd be. I'll go with you.'

'It says *smallest*.' Michael wanted to do the deed alone.

'Smallest *one*. One what? One girl. I'm going with you,' Em said.

'Listen then.' Carrie knelt in front of them, and put her face close to theirs, like Mother when she wanted to say something important. 'You must leave the money where they say, and go away at once. At once, darlings, do you understand?' She even sounded like Mother.

But Michael stuck out his lip and said, 'We'll hide in

that scrap metal dump behind the garage, and when they come for the money, we'll see who they are, you see.' Too young to understand properly the mortal danger Valentina was in, he was getting very excited over the adventure. 'And then I can spot them in the idensity parade.'

'There won't be an identity parade,' Rudolf told him. 'They won't be caught, unless we can call in the police. And if we do that, my poor Val, my poor beloved girl—'

He covered his face with his long bony hand for a moment. Then he pulled himself together, shook back his shoulders, reached for his hat, and said, 'I must go and try to raise the cash. God knows how, but I'll try. You all stay here. Do nothing. These criminals are probably desperate and dangerous. Stay here and lock the doors and windows. Promise me.'

They did not say Yes or No. Carrie and Lester had exchanged the message of their secret look, expressionless, unblinking. As soon as Rudolf left, they were going to start searching for Aunt Val. *Poor Val, my poor beloved girl.*

They had never thought of her as anyone's beloved girl. But she was, and she might die.

twenty-nine

'She might be dead already,' Lester said, as he and Carrie hurried out to the stable.

Val dead. Lively, noisy, highly coloured, ridiculous Valentina dead, the clucking, clacking voice silenced for ever?

Since she disappeared, Carrie had been forgetting the bad things about her, remembering the good things. There weren't many, but those were what she remembered.

The crust on her steak and kidney pies, with the thick gravy seeping out under the pastry flower in the middle. The way she drove a car, fast and reckless, singing songs from her giddy youth, and yelling at other drivers. Even the giant metal rollers in her hair at breakfast, because Val banging about the kitchen in a shocking-pink housecoat and rollers meant bacon and sausages and fried bread.

Normally, Carrie dreaded hearing the voice or the heels approaching, because they spelled trouble. But now she would give a year of her life to see Val racket through the stable yard, kicking out at hens, and wrinkling her nose at the manure heap.

Someone was coming through the yard. The Vicar climbed over the broken wall from the back field path, wearing baggy slacks and a rough old sweater, but still looking like a vicar.

'Where's Rodge?' he called, as Carrie looked over John's half door.

'He went to the church.'

'He didn't. I've been waiting there. Not like him to forget.'

'He was worried about—' Carrie began, and stopped.

To tell the Vicar about Rudolf's fake accident would

mean telling him about the kidnapping, and that would be as bad as telling Arthur. The Vicar would broadcast it from the pulpit, *and* tell the police.

'About what?' he asked, but Carrie changed the subject by bringing John out and mounting. Lester got on Peter bareback, by his patent method of sitting behind the ears and sliding down the neck when the chestnut raised his head.

'Bit late to go riding.' The Vicar looked up at the darkening sky, where clouds were closing down the day. 'Where are you going?'

'Oh – round about.'

Val might have managed to throw something out of the kidnap car – a scrap of paper from her handbag, a handkerchief, a hairpin, one of her big red nerve pills – when she realized that she was not being taken to the hospital. A chance in a million, but they were going to search the local roads, looking for clues.

They waited impatiently for the Vicar to leave, but he said, 'Give me a lift back then, Carrie. My knee's playing me up.'

He stepped on to Michael's mounting block, and put a leg across John's back behind the saddle. They rode through the fields and across the patch of waste ground where children built forts and tunnels. Because of these hazards, Wendy always took Rodge along the same path through here when they went to the church. Now some joker had built an elephant trap across that path.

'Gregory Ferris,' Lester said. 'I know his style.' He knew the specialities of all the local boys. 'Good thing Rodge did forget to go to the church. He could have broken a leg.'

While Lester got off to clear away the branches and fill in the hole, Carrie and John took the Vicar through the gap in the hedge and down the bank into Church Lane.

The Vicar went into the church to turn off the lights and lock up. Carrie waited for Lester by the churchyard wall. Grey gravestones glimmered in the half light, the older ones leaning, as if they had got tired of commemorating people no one was alive to remember.

In the far corner of the wall, she could just make out the curve of the angel's wings over Charlotte Fraser's grave, and her hand went of its own accord to the locket round her neck, which held John's picture and the small curl of Charlotte's hair.

It had brought her luck once, at the circus when they had rescued Roy.

Help me to rescue Val. Bring me luck again.

On an impulse, Carrie rode to the unlatched gates. John pushed one side open with his nose and shoulder, and they went in, and threaded their way between the tombstones to the corner of the wall where the angel wept over 'our beloved little daughter'.

Bring me luck again.

The evening wind stirred in the tops of the trees, and the Vicar clanged shut the iron gates.

Shut the gates! He had locked up for the night, and shut Carrie in. 'Hey!' She went to the gate, swerving John round tombstones, and saw the back of the Vicar's car driving away.

The wall round the churchyard was too high to jump. So was the fence at the bottom of the vicarage lawn. Carrie shouted, but there were no lights in the vicarage. Nothing.

Carrie began to shout for Lester, the old stones of the church returning the vibrations of her scared voice. It was getting dark. She was locked in, trapped and helpless, among the dead.

'Lester!'

'You rang?'

Beyond the stone curve of the angel's wing, Peter's head appeared, then Lester.

'Come on out, quick,' he called. 'That dog barking miles away—'

'I didn't hear it.' But Lester could see and hear and smell farther than anyone.

'It was Wendy. Something's happened. Come on, quick.'

'I can't—' Carrie began, but he had swung Peter round to ride back to the road.

John trampled, and called after Peter. The tomb with the angel was lower than the top of the wall on either side. If they were going to jump, it would have to be here. It was a high jump and wide, over the tombstone slab and over the angel.

Peter's hoofs clacketted out on to the road, trotting away fast. Carrie turned John, and gave him as much run as she could on the path between the graves. One – two – and he stood back and took off over the tomb, over the angel. The white curve of the wings flashed below, and they landed, they were free, and John turned like a whip to follow Peter.

Lester had pulled over to the grass verge, and was cantering far ahead. He turned, and swung his arm at Carrie, and she galloped after him along the edge of the straight old Roman road that ran like an arrow towards the darkening hills.

thirty

'Where were you?' Lester pulled up.

'Locked in. We jumped out over Charlotte Fraser's angel.'

'Some jump!' He turned back to grin at her, and Carrie said, 'It was John, not me, he—'

'Listen.' Lester turned his face into the wind. The horses raised their heads and pricked their ears.

'I thought I heard ... Wendy!' Lester called.

There was nothing. Beyond the hedges, the greening wheat fields lay still and shadowed. There were no houses on this part of the road, only some old buildings left when the smaller farms were taken over by the wheat combine. Very few cars came this way, into the hills, because there was a quicker road through the valley.

'Wendy – speak!'

'You can't have heard her.' Rodge always went to the village. He never walked along this lonely road.

'I did. It was that double bark.' Lester's face was taut and keen, straining into the rising wind that flung spatters of rain.

'Why would Rodge go so far?' Carrie screwed up her face against the rain. 'Is it something about Val?'

'He doesn't know about Val. He thinks she went to the hospital.'

'Why would he come out here? I don't understand. Where is he, Lester? What's happening?'

Carrie felt exhausted and confused. But Lester reached across from his horse and pressed her hand with his thin strong fingers.

'That,' he said, his dark eyes eager for adventure, 'is what we're going to find out.'

* * *

They cantered on down the side of the road. Last time they had cantered together, on the stubble strip at the edge of the long ploughed field, it had been like a fantasy of flying. Tonight it was real, intent with urgency and danger, and Carrie suddenly knew that she and Lester would not dream together again of flying, downstairs or anywhere. Was this the beginning of growing up?

Lester stopped dead, and John ran into him. A rutted, weed-grown track led off to the right through a tangle of trees, overgrown with thorn and bramble hedges. It used to be the drive to a farm house, long since abandoned and falling to ruin.

'Nobody has lived here for years,' Carrie said.

'I saw a light,' Lester whispered, although there was no one to hear.

'You couldn't.'

'Through the trees – look.'

A tiny wink of yellow light as the branches moved.

'Rodge couldn't be *here*,' Carrie said.

'I know, but—' Lester raised his voice and called, 'Wendy!'

They listened. The wind blew the trees like hair, and the horses snorted, getting their breath back after the canter.

'Wendy – speak!'

There it was. Not her clear double bark, because the second part of it was suddenly muffled in a yelp of pain, but unmistakably Wendy.

'I'm going in.' Lester's face was set and grim.

'I'll come with you.'

'No, you stay with the horses.' Lester started down the overgrown track.

'We can tie them in the trees. I'm coming with you,' Carrie said.

'No.'

If it had been anyone else, Carrie would have argued, or gone anyway. With Lester, you let him take charge.

But Carrie did follow him part of the way up the drive, leading the horses between the tangled hedges, to where she could see the house without being seen. It was a small crumbling brick house, part of the roof gone, the chimney fallen into the grass, the windows boarded up or broken, the front door rotted and sagging.

The door was slightly pulled back now on the dark interior, and a man was looking through the opening.

'What do you want?' he called out. 'Who's there?' That voice! Now Carrie remembered where she had first heard it. It was the voice of the man she had stumbled against outside Val's house, and who had cursed her.

Lester walked boldly across the rank grass and weeds that had once been the farmhouse garden. Confronting the man, he looked smaller than usual, but brave.

'I'm selling tickets for the Boy Scouts' picnic,' he said in the clean, innocent voice which he used on his mother when he was up to something secret.

'Get out of here,' the man said hoarsely, 'and take the bloody Boy Scouts with you.'

'Yes, sir!' Carrie saw Lester give the Boy Scout salute, although he had been thrown out of the Scouts for being too bossy. He turned smartly on his heel and walked casually back through the long grass, whistling 'Colonel Bogey' in his clear blackbird's whistle. But as soon as he was out of sight beyond the bushes, he ran.

As Carrie led the horses back to the road, Lester panted out through the brambles with his wet shirt torn and his face scratched.

'He's armed,' he said. 'I saw the gun. They're in there all right. I whistled to let them know we'd found them.'

'Them?'

'That man – I knew his voice.'

'So did I. He was hanging about outside Val's house in London. He heard her say she was coming to World's End.'

'And he's the one who came to tell her about the accident. *Val is in there too.*'

Val and Rodge! Somehow he must have found her. Gentle, timid Rodge in there, helpless, confused, unable to see his captors, Wendy tied up, even killed perhaps – she had obviously been struck when she barked – Val dead . . .

'What are we going to do?' Carrie shivered. Her shirt was soaked and her hair streaked round her face. The rain ran down her cheeks like tears.

'I'm going round to the back of the house,' Lester said. 'It's a rickety place. There may be a way to get them out.'

'But if he's armed – Lester, no! You might get shot.' Carrie grabbed his torn sleeve.

'Not me.' He pulled away. He always thought he couldn't be hurt. When he broke his arm riding Roy, the shock of finding that he was breakable had been worse than the pain.

Carrie grabbed him again. 'Rodge and Val will get shot. Lester, please – it's too dangerous now. We must tell the police.'

'You're right.' He suddenly yielded, took the halter rope, and vaulted on to Peter's back. As Carrie scrambled into John's saddle to follow him, he turned and grinned. 'You're always right, Carrie.'

It was the first time he had ever said that.

thirty-one

After they made the telephone call, they hurried back to the derelict farm through the wet night. They tied up John and Peter in an open cattle shelter across the road, and hid in the loft of the barn near the house, where they could watch and be ready to jump down if they were needed.

The policemen came stealthily to surround the house. Looking through a slit in the high loft door, Carrie and Lester only saw a hint of them – a shadow sliding behind a tree, a bush shaking, a man in uniform creeping through the long grass to crouch behind the kidnapper's car at the side of the house.

The loft ladder creaked, and a policeman's head and shoulders came through the opening in the floor, looking cautiously round. In the darkness, they could not see his face, but when he saw them kneeling by the door, he whispered, 'Who's there?' in the voice of a very young man.

He was holding a rifle. Carrie and Lester turned with their backs to the loft door, as if he were a firing squad. Carrie's throat was too dry to speak, but Lester whispered back, 'It's us. The ones who gave the alarm.'

'Keep back then.' The young policeman crawled over the hay dust of the shaky floor, and lay down on his stomach, with his rifle to the crack in the door. He was very tense, and you could sense the tension outside too, men hidden and waiting, watching the house. The desperate men inside perhaps were watching too, straining their eyes into the darkness.

'Keep back, you kids,' the young policeman muttered again, but he did not look round, so Carrie and Lester crawled to a place where they could see through a space between the rotting boards of the barn.

They held their breath. The black wet night waited. Suddenly everything happened. Spotlights in the bushes flooded the farmhouse with light, and the Scottish voice of an officer behind the car boomed out through a loud hailer.

'This is the police. The building is surrounded. We are armed. We have tear gas and dogs. They will not be used if ye'll free the people ye're holding, and surrender quietly.'

He had a strong Scots accent, magnified by the loud hailer. 'Come out and surr-rrender.'

It was incredibly dramatic. Carrie gripped Lester's arm so tightly that she was gripping the bone.

'We have ye surr-rrounded, ye know. Ye canna ge' away.'

For answer, a single shot pinged against the metal of the car door.

'We're not here fer shoot'n,' the officer called back. 'We're here to save these people's lives. And yours. Will ye talk to an officer? If ye will, he'll come forward un-armed.'

For answer, another shot. It cracked into the car window splintering the glass.

The officer was silent. After the violence of the shot and the shattered glass, the stillness was intense.

As if he could not stand it, the man who had fired called out in a nervous, rasping voice, 'That's what anyone will get who moves. If you attack, we'll kill the man and the woman.'

Val was still alive. Rodge was alive. There was no sound from them, but they were alive. With nerves strung tight as telephone wires, Carrie tried to send thought messages to the house: *Hang on. Be brave. Dear Rodge, be brave. Aunt Val, hang on . . .*

She jumped as Lester jumped, at a slight disturbance in the bushes by the car, and the shot which answered it, splintering another window.

'Will you talk to me?' Not the officer's Scots voice. A very familiar voice, high and breaking with strain and distress.

'This is Rudolf Fielding. I'm begging you. Don't harm my dear – my dear—'

Carrie had never heard a man sob. How strange that it should be cold, controlled Rudolf, who seemed too dried up for tears.

'Don't hurt my dear wife!' he begged like a child.

'Then call off the cops, you————' The man in the house swore back at him.

'Yes, if you will only let her go. You can have the money. It's where you said – all of it. Keep your bargain. I've kept mine.'

'By bringing the bogies,' the man sneered. 'You done it now, old fool.'

'We'll wait.' The Scots officer had taken the loud hailer. His voice was impassive. 'We'll wait until ye're rr-rready to come out.'

No one spoke any more. No one moved. In the hay loft, the young policeman lay on his stomach with his gun in the crack of the door, and his eye along his gun. Outside, the front of the house was floodlit like a stage set. The rain fell silently and steadily in the widening shafts of light.

The Scots officer kept on talking. He waited for answers, but none came. There were no more shots. Occasionally, sounds from inside the house, thuds, steps, a muffled curse, and once, something that sounded like the strong nails of a dog's paw scrabbling at floor boards.

Wendy.

Carrie thought she had only whispered it inside her head, but the young policeman said, 'Shut up!' so fiercely that she thought he might be as scared as she was.

At last, after what seemed a whole night time, or a whole life time, there was a lot of noise behind the front door of the farmhouse, and the man's hoarse voice called, 'We're coming out. Get away from the car. If you shoot, you'll shoot the man and the woman.'

'We'll no' shoot. Come out unarmed.'

The door was dragged open with a wail of rusted hinges. Into the pathway of stabbing light, blindfolded, gagged, their hands tied behind them, Val and Rodge staggered. Two men were at their backs. Stocking masks over their heads made them look like walking dead. One hand pushed a hostage. The other held a gun.

Wendy walked beside Rodge, without her harness, but in her correct Guide Dog place, by his left leg and just in front. Her head was low, and she was limping. As the spotlight moved down to keep the group in the light, Carrie saw that one ear hung torn and bleeding.

'Val!' Uncle Rudolf cried out.

The men swung their guns round, and Rodge stumbled and almost fell.

'Get up, you—' The man behind him jerked him up roughly, and hit the side of his head with the hand that held the gun.

Wendy turned and sprang. She knocked the man to the ground. The gun went off, and the man screamed hoarsely as she stood on his chest, growling like a lion. Policemen dashed from their cover on all sides. The other man let go of Val and ran, ducking back between the house and the car into a net of police.

As they dragged the men away, Rodge sat on the ground holding his head. Val sat on a big stone in the glare of the spotlight. Rudolf knelt to unfasten her wrists and the gag and blindfold. She did not cry or scream. When Carrie and Lester dropped down the ladder and ran out of the barn and across the grass, she was just sitting there like a doll, her hands hanging, her eyes dull and her mouth open, her face with no blood behind it.

'Val, Val – oh my poor Val.' Uncle Rudolf threw his arms round her as if she were his child. Aunt Valentina dropped her tangled head of bedraggled hair and cried like a child on his bony shoulder.

Rodge was incredibly calm. When he was untied, he lifted his head and laughed feebly.

'Bit of a joke,' he said, 'blindfolding a bl- a bl- a blind man.'

Feeling that Wendy was bleeding, he put the cloth blindfold round her head, and tied it under her chin. She sat jammed up against him, like an old lady with toothache.

'They didn't believe I was blind,' he said. 'They thought I was faking.'

'Head all right?' The Scots officer bent down to look at him.

Rodge nodded, then winced, and put up his hand again.

'Ye're a brave man,' the officer said.

'Not brave,' Rodge said, 'just stupid. I was going to the church.' He turned his head to Carrie and Lester. 'Crossing that bit of waste ground, there was something on the path.'

'Gregory Ferris's elephant trap,' Carrie said.

'Good thing Wendy stopped. She took me round it. But then she must have gone the wrong way. She didn't go back to the path. I was confused. So was she. We got lost. We went through a gap in the hedge, and I thought we were on the road to the village, but we went on and on. A car passed us, and it turned off the road and stopped. I went after it – through a jung-jung-jungle or something, nearly tore my beard off. I ran into a house. I mean, I fell over the door step, so I knocked to ask where I was, and before I could say – say – say – Wendy and I were grabbed and chucked inside.'

'I heard her bark,' Lester said.

'I told her to. While they were gagging me, I told her

again, and they hit her. I thought we-we'd had-had-had it. Then I heard you at the door.'

Valentina had stopped crying. She wiped her nose on her sleeve, ran a hand through her wild hair, and stood up. Leaning on Rudolf, she tottered in her town boots over the rough grass to face Rodge.

She looked at him for a moment, and he looked innocently up at her, not knowing who was there.

'I think you saved my life,' she said.

'Oh rot.' Rodge looked down, embarrassed. 'It was because Wendy went the– went the—'

'Wrong way?' Val smiled with her bruised, pale mouth that had lost all its harsh lipstick.

'Remember I said, on the floor in your house,' Rodge looked up again, 'she's not a machine, she's a dog?'

'Thank God she is.' Aunt Val, who hated dogs, bent to lay her hand gently on Wendy's bandaged head. 'She went the right way.'

thirty-two

While Val and Rudolf and Rodge were being taken out to the cars, Carrie and Lester ran through the bushes, and across the road where the police car radios chattered incessantly, to get John and Peter out of the cattle shed.

The rain had stopped. As they rode back towards the village, the sky was already lightening behind the church spire and the chimneys. No one was up yet. They clattered through the empty streets and out on to the Wake road, where the abandoned garage stood at the cross roads, with the petrol pumps pulled out, and bits of rusty iron sticking out of the broken concrete.

From behind the garage, the gaunt hairy shape of Gilbert sauntered out, yawning. On the scrap heap, they found Michael curled up asleep inside a rusted mudguard. Near him, Em slept on a pile of inner tubes, her hair in spirals, like a wet retriever.

In the call box, where the telephone had long ago been yanked from the wall, and the coin box smashed in, the envelope with Uncle Rudolf's money was under a stone on the floor.

'Blood money.' Lester picked it up and held it out to Carrie. She backed away. 'You take it.' Somehow the money seemed contaminated with the violence and horror of this night.

Michael took the envelope. 'It's my responserability.'

Carrie and Lester put Michael and Em on the horses – in front of them, so they wouldn't fall off if they went to sleep again – and took them home.

Tom was there, and Liza. Liza had put Val to bed, and Tom had poured the last of the brandy Mr Mismo kept for emergencies and birthdays. They were talking about colleges. *Colleges?* Had Rudolf's mind been so unhinged by the crisis that he was going to help Tom to study to be a vet after all? Tom kept looking towards the sofa, where Liza and Rodge held hands across Wendy, who lay between them.

'Are you in love?' Em asked them curiously.

'Knock it off,' Liza said. 'You don't catch me falling for a bloke who can't even see me beautiful face.'

'Might be a good thing,' Em said. 'He'd never know.'

When Michael gave Uncle Rudolf the envelope of money, he took out the notes and counted them suspiciously.

Same old Rudolf, they were thinking, but then Rudolf, without changing the niggardly expression his face always wore when he handled money, held out one of the notes to Michael, one to Em, one to Carrie, one to Lester. Hundred pound notes. One by one, they climbed on the kitchen table, and put the money in the hanging red crock.

'Saving World's End.' Uncle Rudolf squinted up at the label. 'You can cut that down for a start. You're too late.'

They stared. The heroic excitement of the night ran out into their feet, a burden of misery, weighing them down for ever.

No one spoke. Finally Carrie heard herself say in a tiny voice like a whispered croak, 'You-you sold this place?'

'I've given it away.' Uncle Rudolf paused for an eternity. 'To you. Not to that feckless father of yours. He'd gamble it away, or set fire to it, or let it get dry rot.'

'It's got dried rot,' Michael said.

'I'm giving it to all of you – Tom, Carrie, Em, Michael – because of what you did tonight. I'm giving you World's End.'

Monica Dickens

Other books in the World's End series are also in Piccolo

The House at World's End 20p
Summer at World's End 20p
World's End in Winter 25p

The Fielding children, Tom, Carrie, Em and Michael, fend for themselves in a tumbledown country pub and have all the fun, freedom and thrilling adventures they could wish for.

Follyfoot 35p
Dora at Follyfoot 30p

Callie, Dora, Steve and all the residents of the Follyfoot stables in two books based on the ever-popular Yorkshire Television series.

and for younger readers

The Great Escape 25p

This exciting tale is set in Paris at the time of the bloody revolution. Dangerous and thrilling, you can't put the book down.

The Great Fire 25p

Set against the tragedy of the Great Fire of London, this thrilling story is not only packed with excitement but is also an excellent introduction to historical stories.

Rudyard Kipling

The Jungle Book   50p
The Second Jungle Book   50p

First published in 1894 and 1895, the Jungle Books have
delighted countless people with the tales of Mowgli, Toomai,
Rikki-Tikki-Tavi, Baloo and Bagheera. Fables illustrating
profound truths, they are also thrilling and exciting stories.

Puck of Pook's Hill   50p
Rewards and Fairies   50p

These two volumes of the stories of Puck and the amazing things
he reveals to the children Dan and Una make exciting reading as
Puck confronts them with some very interesting people . . .

Just So Stories   40p

These delightful stories tell you fascinating things like How the
Leopard got his Spots, How the Camel got his Hump, and How
the Alphabet was Made. This enchanting book is one of
Rudyard Kipling's most famous.

Piccolo Non-Fiction

Piccolo All-The-Year-Round Book 50p
Deborah Manley

Collecting Things 30p
Elizabeth Gundrey

Amazing Scientific Facts 25p
Jane Sherman

**Blue Peter Special Assignment:
Venice and Brussels** 25p
Dorothy Smith and Edward Barnes

**Blue Peter Special Assignment:
Madrid, Dublin and York** 25p
Dorothy Smith and Edward Barnes

Piccolo Encyclopedia of Sport 40p
Peter Mathews

Piccolo Encyclopedia of Useful Facts 40p
Jean Stroud

These and other Piccolo books are obtainable from all booksellers and
newsagents. If you have any difficulty please send purchase price plus
7p postage to

PO Box 11 Falmouth Cornwall

While every effort is made to keep prices low, it is sometimes
necessary to increase prices at short notice. Pan Books reserve the right
to show new retail prices on covers which may differ from those
previously advertised in the text or elsewhere.